WICKED AMBITIONS

D1415154

Reginald K. Write

www.ReginaldWrite.com

CHAPTER 1

"Take that shit, nigga," Max commanded, staring down into my eyes. We'd been going at it for a minute in mad positions, and I now found myself pinned to the bed in the missionary style with my legs over his broad shoulders. "You love this dick, don't you?"

"Hell yeah. You know I do," I breathed, barely able to speak. Dude's pipe game was no joke. "Fuck me, yo." I gripped my hard dick and started furiously jacking it. I was close. "I'm 'bout to--" Before I could even finish my sentence, I bust a fat nut all over my chest.

"That's what I'm talking about." Max grinned and lowered his sweaty muscular body on top of me, pushing my knees back towards my head so he could get all the way up in my guts. The platinum medallion which hung from his neck rested on my chest causing a chill to rush through me as it touched my skin. However, that cold sensation was quickly replaced with waves of pleasure as Max started plunging his full length into me, making my eyes roll back in my head. I grunted and gritted my teeth. His strokes were getting faster and harder. I could tell he was on the edge.

"Come on, bust that shit, baby," I encouraged.

He sat up on his knees and pulled out of me. He hastily rolled off the condom and started jacking his dick, his abs and arm muscles flexing with each pump. After a few strokes, his shit spat three ropes of hot cum on my stomach. He just stayed in that position, breathing hard and squeezing out the last drop. A satisfied smile spread across his face before he leaned in and kissed me. We laid there like that, covered in sweat and cum, neither of us disrupting the post-sex high. Aside from the faint sound of a random car horn honking somewhere on the streets below, the room was totally silent. I basked in the peace and quiet. I felt so content at that moment. Just me and my boy. No headaches or worldly worries. I gently stroked his clean-shaven head. He shifted a little and let out a deep sigh, the way he always did when he had something on his mind.

"What's the matter?" I asked.

"I gotta meet with that nigga Scorch this week." Shameek "Scorch" Sampson was the head of Max's record label and his boss. "He's thinking about signing some new cat, but he wants me to hear his stuff first."

"Oh, word?" I replied, trying not to sound too eager. "He's looking for new talent?"

"That nigga always looking for someone or something to make him more money," he grumbled.

"So, uh…you change your mind yet about what I asked you before?" I hadn't ventured to broach this topic in a minute, but since he'd brought it up, I figured it might be worth a shot to throw it out there again.

"Nope."

I sucked my teeth in frustration. "Man, why not?"

"Trust me, you don't want me to do it, bae." He wrapped me in his arms and rubbed his nose in the nook of my neck like a cat, his goatee tickling my skin. "From the outside, things may look sweet; but there's a lot of grimy, gritty shit you don't see. There's a price to pay for everything. I wanna protect you from all of that." His full lips kissed my cheek and then whispered in my ear, "I'll take care of you, son. Just stick with me, and you'll always eat."

Once again, Max (or "Madd Maximus," as he was known in the music industry) had shot me down. I twisted my lips. "I don't wanna eat off your plate for the rest of my life. I wanna cook my own food, yo." I laughed and then got serious again, turning my head to meet his gaze. Even though he'd broken me off with paper plenty of times without me even asking, I wasn't satisfied with that. I wasn't a charity case. I didn't want to be treated like some bitch or bum nigga he had to take care of. "You know I can carry my own weight. All I need is a shot. Baby, just introduce me to him and I'll take it from there."

He sighed and pulled away from me. Sitting upright on the bed, he placed his feet on the floor. "Nah, I already told you a thousand times I'm not doing that."

It was more like a thousand and one times.

"That's fucked up, bruh." I'd been begging him for months to put me on, giving him mixtapes to pass along to his boss. Hearing him throw cold water on my aspirations again set me off. "Damn, it's not like I'm asking you to suck the dude's dick or anything!" I snapped at him. "I just want you to give him some of my shit to listen to so he can make up his own mind!" I was getting some nice buzz off my mixtapes, but it was all underground. Hood love was good and all, but that shit wasn't goin' to put any money in my pockets or any shoes on my little boy's feet. I needed to be signed to a major label to make my dreams come true.

"I told you, Wicked," he said, addressing me by my street/rap name, "I'm not going to do it, so you might as well drop the subject." His calm, resolute tone had pissed me off. Despite both of us being only a year apart and in our early twenties, it seemed as though he was treating me like his spoiled little girl having a tantrum. That shit pissed me off even more.

"Why not?! Fuck you scared for? All you gotta do is casually slip him one of my CD's and say, 'Aye, I want you to check out one of my homies…this nigga right here fire, yo'." I grinned, making puppy dog eyes. "Hell, you don't even have to say you know me, if that's what you're worried about." I could understand him being leery of mixing business with pleasure, but that didn't mean he couldn't help me out. Hell, if the shoe had been on the other foot, I wouldn't have thought twice about doing the same for him.

He lit a blunt and took a deep pull. Exhaling smoke from his nostrils, he frowned. He got up from the king-size bed without saying anything and walked across the room. Besides the gold necklace with the platinum dragon medallion resting against the smooth, caramel-complexioned skin of his broad muscular chest, he was butt ass naked. I shifted on the comforter and sat up, propping myself on the fluffy pillows against the headboard to get a better look at his 6-foot-2 frame. No matter how many times I had seen Max naked, I still couldn't help admiring his perfect, lean swimmer's physique. For a total top, he had one of the sexiest bubble butts I'd ever seen. He stood at the ceiling-to-floor window with his arms folded, looking down on the city. The moonlight reflecting through the window showcased his sculpted contour. The view of his muscled back and hairy ass almost rivaled the penthouse view of Manhattan. Whenever he walked away from me and went quiet, it meant the case was closed, and the conversation was over. I knew dude like the back of my hand. We'd been fucking around on the low for years, even while we both lived in the hood. I'd known him long before he'd blown up and become rich and famous. Way before he'd signed with Scorcher Records and became its hottest in-house producer, collabing with and creating hits for all the members of the Fiyah Spitta Team.

I huffed in frustration. Even though I knew I was treading on dangerous ground by pushing the issue, I didn't care. I was hungry and confident. "It's not like he's gonna know we fucking just because you mention my name or introduce us, son!"

"NO!" He growled, spinning around to shoot an angry glare in my direction. "JUST DROP IT, OKAY?!" The platinum emblem on his neck shimmered in the moonlight as his chest rose and fell. He let out a long breath as if he were trying to calm himself and regain his composure.

Fuck. Now you done went and pissed him off, dumb ass, I chided myself. Getting him angry definitely wasn't going to get me anywhere. I switched tactics, softening my tone when I spoke again. "You know I'm good — you said it yourself. You weren't just blowin' smoke up my ass when you said that shit, were you?"

"Of course not." He walked back to the bed, his dick swinging like a pendulum with each step he took. He sat down and gently caressed my face with his strong hand. "You know I think you're a lyrical genius and a beast on the mic."

"So why don't you set up a meeting with the man then???" I interrupted, my voice full of exasperation again.

He shook his head and took another pull of the blunt, letting the smoke fill his lungs. He then snuffed it out in the ashtray on the nightstand and turned to me. His deep set eyes were red and glassy as he peered into mine. "All I'm going to say is, being under contract to that dude ain't all it's cracked up to be. Trust me on this."

"Yeah, well, I'll take that contract any day, son," I sniffed. "I'd rather work for that nigga Scorch than continue to hustle on the streets and shit."

"No you don't." He smiled grimly and kissed me on the forehead. "I already told you that you wouldn't be a good fit there. All the cats at that label rap about is a bunch of meaningless garbage. You don't belong in that sort of environment. You're better than that."

Although I considered myself a "conscious" rapper who didn't glorify drugs and violence, that didn't mean I couldn't switch up my style in a way that would impress Scorch, while still staying true to myself. I knew the "not a good fit" line was just another lame excuse. I looked away and tried to hide my frustration, however, I was bad at concealing shit. I wore my emotions on my face and my heart on my sleeve. I wanted to say more, but I knew it was a dead issue. For whatever reason, Max wasn't going to budge, and I knew how stubborn the nigga could be once he made up his mind.

"Stop pouting, bae. You look like my lil' girl when she can't get her way." Lifting my chin with his fingers, he leaned in to place his lips on mine. Although I was pissed at him, I couldn't help but get turned on as he aggressively kissed me. My dick began to rise. I moaned and laid back as he worked his way down my body, first sucking my nipples and then trailing his way down my abs. By the time he'd gotten to my dick, it was standing at full attention again. He gripped it in his hand and began licking his tongue around the head. I hissed and closed my eyes, preparing to feel the warm wetness of his mouth. Just as his lips engulfed me, his phone rang, prompting him to stop.

I cursed under my breath and opened my eyes.

He grabbed his phone from the nightstand, looking at the screen. "See what I mean? This somebody from the team now." I looked over his shoulder, watching him enter his passcode, just as I'd done many times before. *0512*. It was an easy code to remember due to its sad significance (it was the month and year his grandmother had passed away). A deep frown creased his face as he rose from the bed. "I gotta take this, bae. I'll be back in a minute."

As I watched him leave the room to talk business in another part of the apartment, I was a little discouraged, but undeterred. I knew I was talented. I knew I would blow up if given the chance to reach the masses. I just had to make it happen.

A short while later, I heard the sound of running water. Maximus came back in the room and placed his phone back on the stand. He removed his necklace and set it down also. "Aye, I gotta roll out in a minute."

"Really?" I tried not to sound too disappointed. "What's up?"

"Something came up and I gotta take care of it ASAP." He seemed a little tense.

"Everything okay?"

"Yeah...it's nothing. I'm 'bout to jump in the shower. You going to join me?" He bit his bottom lip in that sexy way only he could.

"Yeah, I'll be there in a minute."

"Aight. Don't keep me waiting." He smiled at me and then left the room again.

I waited several minutes before I got up and tip-toed to the door and peered down the hallway. After I made sure he was in the bathroom and the door was closed, I quietly made my way around the bed. Taking a deep breath, I snatched up his iPhone and hastily punched in his passcode. I scrolled through his long ass list of contacts which contained the names and phone numbers of rappers, producers, and other industry types until I found what I was looking for. I felt a twinge of guilt over what I was planning; I pushed it out of my mind. I'd been mulling this plan over for months now, but I'd always managed to talk myself out of it. However, after this convo, I realized there was no other way. I had to do what I had to do, consequences be damned. I had bills to pay and a kid to feed. I couldn't keep on strugglin' and strivin' out here. If Max didn't care about me enough or have enough faith in me to help me achieve my dreams, then I would just have to do it without him.

One way or another, Wicked was going to get his.

CHAPTER 2

I walked into my house to find a plate of pork chops under a sheet of aluminum foil sitting on the countertop. I grabbed one and put it in my mouth. Just as I bit into it, my mother came into the kitchen carrying her pocketbook.

"I thought I heard you come in."

"You look nice. Where you going—a hot date or a booty call?" I asked, smiling.

"Mind your business." She pulled the strap of her purse over her shoulder. "What you *need* to be worried about is your half of the rent that I still haven't gotten yet."

"Yeah, ma. I know, I know. I got you tomorrow."

"Mmhmm." She pointed at the open envelops scattered on the table. "And feel free to pay a bill or two while you're at it."

I sighed. We had this same damn talk every other day. I already knew where the conversation was headed.

"So, any luck on getting a *real* job today?"

"Ma, how many times I gotta tell you--I already have a 'real' job? I'm not just doin' this music thing for shits and giggles." It wasn't like I never had a legit gig before. I'd worked as a mover, a janitor, hell, even as a security guard. Ordinary, mundane shit like that wasn't for me though. No disrespect to peeps who did those types of jobs, but I always knew in my heart I was destined for more.

"I understand you have lofty goals, but you're 22 now, Will. How much longer are you going to pursue this pipedream? Just because Max lucked out and made it, that doesn't mean you will."

I frowned. "It's not a 'pipedream.' I gotta plan to make my dream a reality. Just watch."

She just stared back at me with an apathetic expression. I'd seen the same look on my baby mother's face plenty of times, too. "That's the same thing your father used to say." Comparing me to my deadbeat dad was the ultimate insult, but I chose to ignore her slick remark. I didn't feel like goin' there with her tonight.

"You'll see. Once I get famous and paid, I bet you'll be the first one with your hand out askin' for somethin'."

"You damn right. After all these years supporting your ass, I better not have to ask either." She started for the door. "Anyway, there's some potato salad in the refrigerator. Make sure you clean up in here after you finish eating. I'll see you tomorrow. Hopefully when I come in, you'll be up bright and early looking for a *real* job."

"G'night, ma," I said, rolling my eyes. *Nag, nag, nag.* I closed and locked the door behind her. I knew she was only lookin' out for me and trying to show me "tough love," but I hated the way she always felt it necessary to dump on my dreams in the process.

After I ate, I sat in my cramped bedroom with my phone in my hand, staring vacantly at the black screen. We'd just celebrated the start of a new year a few days earlier, and here I was still in the same financial predicament I'd been in since I was a teenager. My mother was right; I was gettin' older by the day, and I was still no closer to achieving my dreams. I had to make somethin' happen, pronto. All the way on the train ride home, I contemplated what I was about to do, considering the possible consequences of my actions. If I went through with this, there was no doubt in my mind that it would likely destroy my relationship with Max. *Am I willing to lose him to achieve my goals?* I asked myself. We'd been boys since we were little niggas. But we'd been a lot more than just boys for several years now. I could still vividly remember when everything changed between us and things went to a whole 'nother fuckin' level.

It was a late night in November. Once his mom had gone to work and Max had the crib to himself, I took a cab to his place so we could smoke and chill for a minute. Getting out the cab, I walked up the stairs of the Bedstuy brownstone where he lived, carrying a big ass box under my arm like I worked for UPS and shit. I rang the doorbell and waited for him to answer. A few seconds later, Max opened the door and unlocked the security door. He had no shirt on, just some gray sweats. Even at that age, his body was well defined. His chest was muscular and his abs were all cut up, a prominent v-line disappearing into the waistband of his sweats.

"What's that?" He asked, eyeing the package under my arm.

"Damn, nigga, you ain't gonna invite me in first?"

He laughed. "Oh, my bad, fam." He stepped to the side to let me enter, closing and locking both doors behind me. We stood in the foyer. "So what is it?"

"You sure is an impatient, eager ass, ain't you?" I joked, getting a kick out of delaying the big reveal. "Come on, let's go up to your room."

I followed him up the stairs to his messy ass bedroom, where he closed the door.

"Happy belated birthday, mah dude."
He'd just turned 19 a few days earlier. I handed
him the box. When he saw it, his face lit up like a
jack-o-lantern.

"Oooh, shit!" He exclaimed, dropping to
his knees and tearing into the box. When he
finally finished ripping out the packing material
and saw what it was, he looked up at me with
the widest smile on his face I'd ever seen.
"Where'd you get this from, son?"

I grinned. "Don't worry about all that,
nigga. I got my ways."

"Dayum—I've been lookin' at these
things online," he said, rubbing his hand over
the pricey beat machine. "This had to cost close
to six hundred bucks!"

"Yeah, that's that real professional shit
right there, boy."

He pulled it out of the box and set it on
his lap, marveling at it. He glanced up at me
again. "For real though, how'd you cop this?"

"Don't worry about all that, my nig.
When you rich and famous and making beats for
Jay and everybody else, just remember how I
hooked you up." I laughed.

"No doubt. You know I got you for this.
That's my word, yo." He stood up and excitedly
extended his hand to me, gripping mine and me
pulling into a bro-hug. "Ain't nobody ever did
no shit like this for me before, mah dude." I
could hear the sincere gratitude in his voice.

"Don't even worry about it, fam." I pulled back and smiled at him, still gripping his hand. "Just don't go getting all emotional on me and shit."

He chuckled. "Fuck you, nigga."

After hooking the machine up to his computer, Max spent hours messing around with it, eagerly figuring out what all it could do. I sat on his bed just watching him go crazy and wild out every time he discovered something new. I got a kick out of watching my boy act like a kid with a new toy on Christmas day. Seeing him so happy, made me happy. I loved this nigga like a brother. When he didn't have and I did, I would do for him — and vice versa. We always looked out for one another.

Max was a street nigga, but not to the degree I was. He was always more book smart than anything. Ever since we were little niggas, it was our dream to work in the music industry; mine as a rapper and his as a producer. Whenever we weren't in school or running the streets together, we spent hours at each other's cribs listening to music by our favorite artists and trying to create our own. He would use a basic program to create simple beats on his computer while I scribbled verses on the notepad I always carried around with me. Because I had a sick flow and a wicked way with words, I adopted the name "Wicked". I came up with the name "Madd Maximus", as a play on his name of course, and because I knew with the right equipment, he could be a fuckin' mad genius in the beat making department. When I offhandedly repped him in a rhyme by that moniker, he instantly liked it and went by it from that day forward.

Wicked Will and Madd Maximus. The wave of the future. We were destined to be them new niggas who were goin' to have shit on lock. Together, we were going to conquer the world of Hip-Hop and make it our bitch.

"Aye, get off that for a second and come smoke this shit with me, bruh," I said, finally starting to feel ignored. Max reluctantly tore himself away from his desk and joined me on the bed.

"Damn, man, I love this thing. I still can't believe you did something like this for me." He was all teeth.

"Like I said before, don't even sweat it. If I was the up-and-coming producer, I know you would've done it for me, nah mean?" I sparked the blunt, took a pull and then passed it to him.

He took a hit and remained quiet for a second, staring into my eyes. "Honestly, though, where did you get it, man?"

I sighed. "Don't worry about all that. I did what I had to do."

His eyebrow went up as he handed the blunt back to me. "This shit ain't stolen, is it?"

I grinned and shrugged my shoulders nonchalantly. "I won't tell if you don't tell." I let him believe I'd stolen the equipment. In reality, I'd been saving up for months, hustling and shit in the streets to get up the cash to buy the machine for him legit. However, I wasn't going to let him know that. I had a hardcore reputation and image to uphold. Even though he was my boy, it would've looked mad suspect and soft on my part to be buying another nigga something so expensive.

"Man, I hope you ain't gonna have no cops kicking down my door and shit? If my momz has to bail me out of jail, I'm coming to fuck you up."

I nearly choked on the smoke, coughing and laughing at the same time. When I finally regained my composure, I replied, "Trust me, mah dude--you straight. You ain't got nothin' to worry about."

He eyed me warily for a second, his face slowly softening as he held my gaze. "For real though, you have no idea how much this shit means, Wicked. You didn't have to do this for me."

"For the last time—don't mention it, aight? You know you my boy." I took another pull of the blunt and passed it to him, our fingers gently grazing as he took it from me. I closed my eyes, letting the weed take hold of me. As it started to transport me to another state of consciousness, I suddenly felt a soft pair of lips kiss mine. My eyes popped open to see Max's face an inch from my nose. He wore an uncertain expression, as if he were bracing himself for my reaction. I just blinked, my mind trying to process what had just happened. Was I fuckin' hallucinating, or had my boy just kissed me?

"What the fuck, yo?!" I shoved his chest, pushing him out my face. I jumped up from the bed, my heart racing.

"Will, man, I," Max stammered, his expression a mixture of shock and embarrassment.

"What kinda gay shit you on, bruh???"

"Fuck." He buried his head in hands. "I...I'm sorry for doing that. I don't know what I was thinkin'."

I glared at him. "On some real shit, you dead to me right now, yo." My burning gaze lingered on him for a minute. Judging by the look of anguish and guilt on his face, I could tell my words had cut him deep. I shook my head in disgust and marched to the door.

"Wicked, hold up. Just listen to me for a second." I heard the mattress squeak, and then felt a hand grab me before I could reach the doorknob. I snatched my arm from his grasp.

"Don't put your hands on me, son!" I swung around and punched him in the face. He stumbled back a little and touched the spot I'd hit, staring at me in wide-eyed disbelief. "Fuckin' faggot ass!"

As soon as those words left my mouth, the disbelief on his face was replaced with disdain. Before I could say another word, he charged at me, grabbing me by my hoodie and slamming me back against the door.

"I ain't no damn faggot, yo!" He snarled, his nostrils flaring. "Don't you ever call me that shit again. You hear me???"

"Fuck, you," I spat. I tried to push him off me, but he wouldn't budge. We peered into each other's eyes with equal intensity and hostility. I wasn't a little nigga by any means, but Max had me beat in the height and weight department by several inches and about 30lbs. I was 5'10, a buck 50. He was 6'2 and had to be around 180. "That's what you are, right?"

He shook his head. "You know I don't get down like that."

"So what the fuck you call kissin' another nigga on the lips, then, huh?" I scoffed.

He clenched his jaw, his eyes riddled with confusion. "I...I don't know. I just..." He paused as if trying to gather his thoughts and sort through his emotions. "It's something about you that I've always been drawn to. I don't know what it is, Will, but I just..." He trailed off and drew in a deep breath, looking away. "I don't even know how to explain the shit without sounding suspect." He was at a loss for words, but he didn't need to say anything more. I already knew what he was trying to say and what he was clearly feeling.

Because I felt it, too.

While I'd always had something of a crush on him, I was too afraid to ever admit it to myself for fear of what it meant. I'd fought and tried my damnedest to bury that shit deep inside. And now he was pulling it out of me, bringing all those unwanted desires and emotions to the surface.

I was mad.

Mad at him for forcing me to confront those urges.

Mad at myself for even feeling this way about another dude.

I looked away, not wanting to make eye contact again because I was scared of what might happen if I did. I was breathing hard, my heart hammering against my chest. I knew he was looking at me. I could feel his probing eyes watching me. I could feel his warm breath on my skin. I could feel his hard dick through his sweats pressed against my thigh. Something about the rawness of our emotions and the rush of being physically restrained and dominated by Max was turning me on like a motherfucker. I felt my own shit instantly get on brick in my jeans. I forced myself to slowly look up and meet his gaze.

Our eyes locked onto each other. Time froze. The breath caught in my throat.

In an instant, we started kissing as if we were trying to devour each other, tongues and teeth clashing. Our hands frantically and hungrily roamed all over one another's body. I couldn't believe what we were doing, but I couldn't stop. I didn't want to. Feeling the hardness of Max's body, the pure want and aggression behind his kiss — the shit was mind-blowin'. At that moment, all I wanted to do was give in to him.

We crossed a line that night, saying and doing things to each other that neither of us ever imagined. After we were done, he sat in his chair butt naked and began working on a sick beat that he jokingly dedicated to us. He titled it "Upheaval," because that's what had just happened to our lives. It was rough, but after it was later polished, that was one of the beats that eventually caught the attention of someone in the Fiyah Spitta camp, and ultimately opened the door for him to meet and sign with Scorch himself.

Three years later, that nigga had a state-of-the-art production studio full of expensive audio and recording equipment at his fingertips. And what did I have? No money. No record deal. Nothing but empty fuckin' promises. Things weren't supposed to turn out this way. We were supposed to be a team. A dynamic duo and shit. Now that he'd gotten his, he was basically shittin' on mine. I felt stupid. I felt betrayed. I felt angry.

"You know what?" I said to myself. "Fuck that selfish ass nigga."

I took a deep breath, suppressing any lingering doubts I had. My phone's screen lit up as I turned it on and entered my passcode. I scrolled through my contacts until I found the new entry. I hit call. The number began dialing. It rang three times before a deep voice answered.

"Hello?"

"Is this Scorch?"

"Yeah...who's this?"

"My name's Will Marshall, but I go by the name 'Wicked." My tone was confident and assertive.

A moment went by before he replied. "Wicked, the rapper?"

"Yeah, one and the same," I replied, encouraged by the fact he already knew who I was.

"How did you get this number?"

"I'm a resourceful and ambitious cat, I have ways to get what I want when I need it," I said, feeling myself big time at that moment. "But that ain't really important, mah dude. What matters right now is what I can do for you."

There was a long, awkward silence on the other end. I was just about to look at the phone to see if he'd hung up on me when he said, "Go ahead…I'm listening."

CHAPTER 3

"Since niggas can't beat me, they try to bite my flow,

From BK to the BX they know ya boy got shit on lock like a CO"

My plan had worked. I'd actually managed to talk myself into a meeting with Scorch. I couldn't believe I was sitting in the lobby of Scorcher Records, the hottest Hip-Hop label in the industry. Shit, I was hella nervous. I felt like I was goin' to a fuckin' job interview or something. Since I wasn't even sure what niggas wore to meetings like this, I opted for a Polo shirt, a pair of jeans, some Timbs, a blazer, and a Yankee fitted — not too dressy, but not too street either. I was pacing back and forth, reciting some of the verses I planned to spit for Scorch.

"Err'body feelin' this kid, I always got 'em screamin' for mo,

All Wicked Will wanna know is where that dough at though"

My phone vibrating against my leg snapped me out of my zone. I pulled it from my pants pocket and looked at the caller ID. I rolled my eyes. "Fuck, this nigga got the wackest timing," I mumbled. I touched the screen, sliding the bar to accept the call. "Hello?"

"What's good my nigga!?" Max's deep voice boomed through the speaker. It had been a few days since we spoke. When I left his crib that night after we fucked, I knew he could tell I was a little salty about him turning down my request to set up a meeting with his boss.

"Nothin' much," I replied nonchalantly. "Just out here grindin'. Why?"

"Just asking. Damn, why you getting all defensive? You been up to something behind my back?" His tone was playful.

"Nah, I just been doin' me, like everybody else."

He sighed. "You still mad about the other night?"

"Nah, I ain't mad," I lied.

"Good. I just don't want you getting mixed up with that nigga, Scorch."

I smirked and thought, *Yeah, I bet you don't.*

"Yo, I got some good news for you, bae." His voice beamed. "I think I can pull a few strings and get you a meeting with an A&R at AMP!"

"Oh, word?" I said drily, unimpressed with his news. It was clearly a token gesture to try and appease me. AMP was a decent label, but everybody knew Scorcher Records was the place where the big boys went to play. It was the major leagues and AMP was the minors. Everybody wanted to be signed to Scorcher. Fuck meeting with some bitchass A&R. I was skipping all the middleman bullshit and going straight to the decision maker himself.

"Excuse me, sir?" The receptionist called out.

"Who was that?" Max asked.

"Uh, the receptionist at this place I'm interviewing."

"You ain't mention nothing about a job interview."

"Yeah, they uh, just called me this morning. Aye, look, I gotta go now. I'll holla at you later." I hung up before he could reply and whipped my head in the pretty sista's direction.

She smiled at me, standing up from her station. "Mr. Sampson will see you now."

"Coo." *Bout fucking time.*

My heart raced as I followed her down a long hallway. Damn, I was nervous as fuck. Not only because I was worried about impressing Scorch, but also because I still felt a little conflicted about goin' behind Max's back like this. *Fuck that nigga and get your damn head in the game, Wicked!* I chided myself. *He got his; now you gotta get yours.* I wiped my sweaty palms on my pants and took a deep breath, psyching myself up and putting my game face on. *This is your big chance! This the moment you dreamt about for years! Everything is riding on this meeting — don't blow it worrying about Max's ass!* We soon stood in front of a large office. The plaque on the door read: Shameek Sampson, CEO.

"Good luck," she mouthed, gripping the handle and giving me a flirtatious smile.

"Thanks, ma." I licked my lips and smiled back.

She twisted the handle and gently pushed the door open. I stood in the entrance looking around in awe as she announced my arrival. The walls were lined with framed album covers and platinum plaques amassed by the Fiyah Spitta crew. Against the far wall sat the man primarily responsible for all of that success, the king maker himself—Shameek "Scorch" Sampson—in the flesh. Behind his desk hung a gigantic canvas oil painting of a dragon, the Fiyah Spitta logo which matched the emblem on Max's chain. He looked up from whatever had his attention on his desk and acknowledged our presence.

"Thanks, Darlene." He leaned back in his chair and smiled. "Come in."

I clenched my jaw and stepped through the threshold to a better tomorrow. I heard Darlene close the door behind me. I just stood there for a moment, relishing the experience. Being in that towering skyscraper overlooking the Manhattan skyline. Standing there in that huge office with glass walls and a sweeping panoramic view of the bustling city below. Looking down on it all from so high above, I felt different, more important. The wealth. The power. The respect. Scorch had it all, and I wanted a piece. As I approached his massive glass-top desk, he stood up. He gave me a firm handshake and a smooth smile. He was a good-looking brother with a clean shaven face, curly hair, thick, silky black eyebrows and piercing, grayish eyes who was dressed to the nines in an expensive-looking designer suit. I always thought the nigga was cute in pictures, but in person he was sexy as fuck. He gestured to one of the chairs in front of his desk. I sat down and he did the same. He just stared at me for a moment, as if sizing me up.

"So...Wicked..." He continued to gaze at me. The longer he remained silent, the more awkward I felt. *What the fuck?* Was he trying to throw me off my game or something?

"Uh, yeah," I replied, not sure of what to say. "I bought a copy of my demo." I held up the CD and waved it in front of my face. "Or, I can spit a few bars off the top of my head if you want?"

"No...that's not necessary. I'm very familiar with your flow. Actually, I've had my eye on you for a minute now." He casually leaned back in his high back leather chair, lacing his fingers behind his head. "To put it bluntly, I've been impressed by what I've seen and heard."

"Word?" I tried to restrain my excitement.

"Yeah. Why else do you think I didn't hang up on you last night?" He smiled a little, revealing a deep pair of dimples. "I've seen underground videos of you freestyling. Everyone I've checked out, you were the hottest dude in the cypher. I've seen some of you battling, too...always sick. I love the intensity. The passion. The wordplay. You can go far in this business." From the way he spoke and carried himself, he was clearly educated. But he didn't seem like some punkass corporate suit or anything. Even though he came across as a professional executive, there was a hardness to him, like he could easily flip the script and get hood if he had to.

"Thanks, mah dude." I had to fight myself to keep from cheesing. I already knew I was good, but hearing it come from him certified it. If anybody knew talent when he saw it, it was him.

Scorch was once an up-and-coming A&R at a major record company. One night at a club for a record release party for a new artist he'd recently signed, a fight broke out and a group of niggas shot up the place. Rumor has it that the shit was drug and gang related. The artist was killed by a shot to the dome. Scorch was hit, too, but he managed to survive and soon went on to leave his A&R job and create his own imprint. All the hype and media attention surrounding him combined to make his label wildly successful. It was like that shit took over the world of Hip-Hop overnight. Every time you turned around, the Fiyah Spitta Camp was droppin' some hot, new shit. Everyone and everything that nigga touched seemed to turn into gold (and platinum).

"I like your hustle, man. I believe you'd make a great addition to my roster."

I stopped breathing and sat up straight in my chair. Was he saying what I thought he was?

"I'd like to sign you."

That's what the fuck I'm talkin' bout! I couldn't hold that big ass Kool-Aid smile back anymore.

"But first, I want to know, how bad do you really want this. How far are you willing to go to be down with this label?"

I gave him a blank look. Was this the part where this nigga was gonna ask me to suck his dick or something? Like everybody else, I'd heard the rumors about how these industry dudes get down. I wasn't about to do no shit like that and have anybody holdin' nothin' over my head. He obviously noticed my confusion, so he clarified himself.

"Are you willing to sacrifice everything to be a part of the Fiyah Spitta Team?"

"Yeah. No doubt." I vigorously nodded my head, not quite sure what he was getting at, and not really giving two fucks. I cranked up my enthusiasm. "I'd rep this crew to the fullest, mah dude! That's my word."

"Good. That's what I wanted to hear. I can tell you're ambitious, and that you will do whatever it takes to get what you want. You're hungry. I like that. Those are the type of people I want around me." He reached in a drawer and pulled out some paperwork. "I already took the liberty of having a contract drawn up. Here, look it over." He placed the papers on the desk and slid them over to me. "I'm sure you'll find the terms of the agreement are quite fair."

After all the years of dreamin' and schemin', I couldn't believe I finally had a real record deal in my hands. My eyes scanned the document. It was a bunch of numbers and legal mumbo jumbo. I wanted to jump over the desk and kiss this nigga. I tried to conceal my excitement. I was happy, but I wasn't goin' to be one of these dumb cats who signed his life away because he didn't take the time to read the fine print and shit. "Woah, thanks, Scorch." I looked up at him. "Not to sound ungrateful or anything, but uh…can I take some time to think about this?"

"Of course. I'll give you till the end of the week to decide. Have a lawyer look it over if you want. Like I said, you'll find the terms of the deal are more than fair for a new artist. Trust me, I'm not going to screw you." He smiled. "Anybody you talk to who works for me knows I'm fair and honest."

I doubted Max would vouch for that. He always bitched about Scorch, but he would never tell me what was supposedly so terrible about him. I realized now the nigga was probably just bad talking him to try to discourage me, and keep me from bugging him about introducing us. *Selfish ass muthafucka.* Well fuck him. I went behind his back and got shit done on my own. That's how a real G handles his business. I had no clue how I was gonna break the news that me and him were about to be labelmates, or how he was gonna take it. I guess I would just have to cross that bridge later.

Me and Scorch talked for a few more minutes before wrapping things up with another handshake and a promise to meet again at the end of the week. He showed me to the door and walked with me through the hallway back to the lobby.

"Aight, Scorch, I'll be in touch, man." As we shook hands one last time, I heard the elevator ding. I turned just in time to see the doors slide open...and Max step out.

CHAPTER 4

Our eyes instantly zeroed in on each other and locked. My blood ran ice cold. *SHIT!* As he approached, the look on his face was a mixture of shock, betrayal, and repressed rage.

"Talk about perfect timing!" I had forgotten there was anyone else there besides us until Scorch said something. He was all smiles. Max wasn't. "Will, I'd like you to meet Maximus."

"Madd Maximus???" I pretended to be surprised (which I really was) and hype about meeting him for the first time. "Ah, shit—I love your work, mah dude! Real talk, I think you the hottest producer on the Fiyah Spitta Team!"

"Thanks," Max replied, his face and voice stoic. He gave me a weak handshake.

"Max, this is Wicked." Shameek patted me on the shoulder. "He's gonna be the newest member of our family…or at least I hope he is." He laughed a little.

"Really?" Max's gaze was so intense I had to look away. I was so shook I could barely breathe. I looked down at my feet, praying Scorch didn't pick up on the tension between us.

"Yeah, I gave him a contract to look over. I was just telling him how he doesn't have to worry about me trying to take advantage of him or anything. Although you've only been with this label for a little less than a year, you can attest to me being a fair person to work for, right?"

Max pulled his burning gaze off of me and turned his attention to Scorch. "Yeah. Mos definitely."

It was hardly a ringing endorsement, but Scorch acted like it was. "See, Will? You don't have anything to worry about. I'm going to look out for you the same way I do for every member of my team." He shook his head and snickered. "Sorry, I'm getting ahead of myself again. That is, *IF* you decide to come aboard. Max, I was just talking about wanting to sign him the other day, too, remember?"

"Yeah." Max diverted his eyes to the floor. "I remember."

"And you said--" Scorch seemed to catch himself before saying something he didn't want to. He quickly rewound the tape and hit play again. "It doesn't matter." I wondered what he was going to say. What had Max said about me? "What's funny though is that a couple days later he hits me up out the blue! Since I don't believe in coincidences, I knew it was a good omen telling me to trust my gut and offer him a deal. I still want to know how you got my number though." He chuckled a little as he looked to me.

"Like I said, I got my ways." I grinned uncomfortably, avoiding eye contact with Max. "A magician never reveals his secrets, yo."

Scorch smiled. "I feel you. I respect a man with a 'Get-it-done-by-any-means-necessary' attitude. As long as you haven't hacked into my pictures and shit, it's all good."

I fake laughed along with him. "Nah, never that."

"But alright, Will, let me let you go. Max and I have some business to discuss. Friday, okay?"

"Oh, sure. No doubt. Aye, thanks again for this opportunity."

"No problem. Hopefully you'll decide to take it. You're like a diamond in the rough--raw and rugged. When I'm done polishing you, your shine is going to be so bright you'll blind the world. Trust me." He placed a hand on Max's shoulder and one on mine. "I already know once I get you two in the studio, you're going to make some fiyah tracks together."

This nigga was pouring it on thick, but at that moment all I could see was dollar signs and my name in lights with "Sold Out" under it outside Madison Square Garden. "That's what's up." I almost smiled until I glanced over at Max. The disappointment I saw in his face made my heart drop. I should've been happy as fuck right then, but I wasn't. "It was good meetin' you, my dude. Stay up."

"Yea, you do the same." Max shook my hand, giving me an icy stare. "I'm sure we'll be seeing each other again real soon."

I still felt shitty when I got off the elevator and made my way out the building. I couldn't get the haunting look I'd seen in Max's eyes out of my head. "Dammit," I muttered to myself. I knew he was eventually going to find out about my meeting with Scorch. I just wished I could've broken it to him a different way. Once I passed the security guards I pushed through the revolving doors outside into the bright midday sun. *Focus, nigga*, I told myself. *I'll deal with Max later.* I already knew the fallout from this wasn't gonna be pretty, especially when he put two and two together and realized I went through his phone to get Scorch's number. Hopefully, he'd be reasonable and at least hear me out. I walked for a few blocks until I found an area of the sidewalk not too congested and noisy. I pulled out my phone and called up my baby mama, Tanieka. It rang a few times and went to voicemail. I exhaled through my nose and dialed her again. This time, she picked up.

"What, Will?" Her tone was curt. Tanieka and I linked up during our junior year in high school. A few months after we had started fucking, she got pregnant. I cared about her a lot, but it definitely wasn't love. The feeling was clearly mutual.

"Damn, why you always gotta answer my calls with a stank attitude?"

"*Because* I'm busy, that's why. Unlike *some* people, I'm at work trying to make money to support my son." She never missed a chance to take a shot at my manhood. Just because I didn't work some bullshit 9-to-5 didn't mean I wasn't hustlin' to take care of my seed. I wasn't some deadbeat nigga that had to be dragged to court for child support and shit. "You act like you the only one providin' for lil' Will."

She let out an irritated huff. "I don't have time for this right now, Wicked. What do you want?"

The reckless way she was talking made me want to just say "forget it" and go off on her ass. However, I managed to restrain myself and give her a free pass. "Guess what?"

Silence.

"I just left Scorcher Records...they offered me a deal!"

"What??? Willie, are you serious?!" She squealed in my ear.

"Dead ass, girl." Hearing her address me with excitement and happiness in her voice for the first time in the longest caused an ear-to-ear smile to spread across my face. "I have the contract right here in my hand."

"You didn't sign it right there on the spot?" She sounded perplexed.

"Nah, I didn't want to be hasty and jump into shit without having someone go over it with me." I paused for a second, feeling hesitant about what I was about to ask. "Um, you think you can take a look at it?" Tanieka was a legal assistant at a Midtown law firm.

"Yeah, alright...that's actually a good idea." She sounded pleasantly surprised that I would act rationally and seek legal advice before signing a binding contract. She really did think I was some fucking lowlife idiot, didn't she? "You still in the city?"

"Yup."

"Okay, I'm about to go on lunch in an hour. We can meet up then."

"Cool."

"Bring the paperwork."

"Aight." I ended the call and started walking in the direction of her office.

*****

Tanieka looked at me from across the table with a big grin on her face. "I can't believe my baby is about to be famous!" She shimmied in her seat, waving the contract in the air like it was a winning lotto ticket. The way she was acting was appropriate since we were sitting in a noisy, ratchet ass Mickey D's.

"Oh, now I'm your baby?" I smirked. "Yesterday I was a 'bum ass nigga.'"

She blushed. "Will, you know I don't mean any of that shit I be saying to you when I'm mad. I just be so stressed sometimes trying to raise my — our — son that I take it out on you. You know I love me some you." Right.

"Girl, stop the bullshit. You be doggin' me out every chance you get. Now that you see ya boy ain't no joke, you all in." I'm not gonna lie, it felt good to rub my success in her face. She was forever doubting me, saying I was wasting my time trying to be rapper and I would never amount to shit. Now I was making her ass choke on a big piece of humble pie.

"Boy, hush. You know it's not even like that." She smiled bashfully, giving me a dismissive wave of her hand. "I always had faith in you, baby. I never doubted for a second you were going to blow up. I always knew you were talented. But sometimes, I just got a little impatient waiting for everyone else to realize it, that's all."

"Sure." I cut my eyes.

"I gotta get back to work in a few minutes. I can't wait till I don't have to worry about going to that job and working for those asshole attorneys," she flicked at the half-eaten cheeseburger in front of her. "You coming by later tonight so we can celebrate?" She placed a hand on top of mine and smiled flirtatiously, batting her eyelashes. We hadn't fooled around in years, now she was acting like she wanted to fuck me right there on the table.

"Nah, I'm probably gonna be busy." I withdrew my hand. Ever since that night Max first kissed me, I'd pretty much lost what little sexual interest I had in her and females in general. "And don't go quitting your job just yet; I still haven't decided if I'm gonna sign or not."

She sat back in her chair, her forehead crinkling. "What do you mean? Why not?"

I sighed. As much as I wanted this, something about the look on Max's face was giving me second thoughts. Why was he so adamant about me not signing with Scorch? "My boy Max don't think I should come to his label."

"You going to listen to him?" Her face scrunched up. She never really cared for Max. Partly because she never understood why I spent so much time with him. "If ya'll were such good friends like you say, he would've been put you on months ago once he got his deal. If you let him fuck up your money, you dumber than I thought." So much for the sweet act. "He just doesn't want you working with him because he knows you'll outshine his ass." She shook her weave. "You better stop worrying about your damn friend and start thinking about yourself and your son, and sign that fucking deal."

I twisted my lips and took a sip of my soda. "We'll see."

"We'll see my ass!" Even though it was loud in the restaurant, her outburst still managed to catch some people's attention, causing them to look our way. "There isn't shit else to see except what's right in front of you, Wicked. I'm no lawyer, but I don't have to be to tell you this is a sweet deal. The big advance, the guaranteed percentage of royalties you'll get— you'd be a damn fool to turn it down." She pushed the contract across the table to me.

I reluctantly picked it up and stared at it. She was right. This deal was everything I'd ever hoped and prayed for. It was my ticket out of the hood and to a better life. I would finally be able to do for myself and take care of my kid, my mom and even Tanieka's shady ass the way I wanted. But I couldn't sign it in good conscience without knowing the truth. I had to know why Max was so against me signing with Scorch. I'd never been able to get him to be straight with me before, but now I had the leverage I needed. If he truly had a legit reason for not wanting me to sign with Scorcher, he now would be forced to tell me. "Like I said...we'll see."

CHAPTER 5

"So in a nutshell, every member of that camp has lost a friend or family member within a year of signing. That shit ain't just coincidence, man. Once you sign, you gotta sacrifice someone close to you to Satan." My boy Ronnie stroked his bushy beard as he spoke. "I wouldn't sign that shit if I was you."

I took a hard look at the blunt I held in my fingers, and then stared blankly at him. "This shit ain't laced with crack, is it? You soundin' type crazy right now, bruh."

He gave me a sidelong glance, the corners of his black lips curling upward. "Aight, keep thinking I'm crazy. That's what THEY want you to believe. Everything I told you is right there on Youtube. Look it up for ya'self. That nigga Scorch is down with the Illuminetti."

I rolled my eyes. "It's 'Illuminati.'" It killed me how cats were always screaming about the Illuminati, but couldn't even pronounce or spell the shit right. "Please tell me you don't actually believe everything you watch on fuckin' Youtube, son?"

"Nah, but this is true though. They even interviewed peeps who collaborated the story."

"You mean 'corroborated'?"

His face crinkled. "Shut the fuck up. This ain't no damn English class. Somebody who knows one of Scorch's baby's mama's boyfriend's cousins said Scorch told her he had a near death experience when he got shot. Instead of going to heaven and seeing God, his ass went to hell and met the Devil. He resurrected him and promised that nigga fame and fortune in exchange for his soul and a steady supply of sacrifices and followers," he said confidently. "Why you think their logo is a fucking dragon?"

I couldn't believe dude was dead ass serious, too. He clearly believed everything coming out of his mouth. This is exactly why I needed to sign this deal, I thought. I needed to get out the hood so I could stop hangin' with people like this who just sat around drinkin' and smokin' all day and watchin' off-the-wall shit on Youtube. *Then again, Max did lose his grandma not long after signing to Scorcher*, I mused. *Jesus, now this nigga got you buggin' out!* I shook my head at myself for indulging in this conspiracy theory BS. I passed on taking another hit of the blunt and handed it back to Ron. I'd come to his place with the intention of smokin' one and getting my head straight before I met up with Max, but listening to his crazy ramblings wasn't helping the cause.

"Aight, mah dude," I said, rising from the sofa. "I'm about to be out."

He finished off the blunt and put it in the ashtray. He then stood up and walked me to the door. "Just remember what I said, bruh; them niggas are everywhere. Stay up."

"Yeah, aight." *Nutcase*. I dapped off with him and left his place, headed to the subway.

I felt on edge when I walked into Max's Upper Eastside building, but I tried not to show it. Like always, I said wassup to Ricardo, the Spanish dude who manned the front desk. Since I came here so often, I had a good rapport with all the security staff. He greeted me back and buzzed Max.

A few minutes later, he gave me the OK to go on upstairs. I dapped Ricardo up and proceeded to the elevator bank. An old white woman in a mink coat was standing there waiting. She gave me a wary look as I approached. When the elevator arrived, I let her get on first. I pushed the button to the 35th floor, she pushed the 24th floor. Once the doors closed, she scurried all the way to the far back corner, clutching her bag like she had a bar of gold in that shit. I smirked and faced forward, looking up at the flickering numbers go higher and higher. When the elevator stopped at the 24th floor, the old bitch practically ran through the doors before they could even open good.

"Have a nice night!" I called out, just to fuck with her head. She turned to me, her face full of fear. I smiled and waved at her as the doors closed. *Scary bitch.* I laughed to myself a little, until the elevator started lurching upward again, making me remember the coming confrontation awaiting me. When I spoke to Max on the phone a few hours earlier, I'd been surprised by how eerily calm he sounded. However, I knew it was just the calm before the storm.

It seemed like the elevator ride took forever. Once it finally came to a stop and the doors opened, I sucked in a deep breath, and then made my way to his crib. I reminded myself I had a good reason to do what I did, and I was going to defend my actions no matter what. This wasn't about me betraying Max's trust, I reasoned. This was about making him reveal why he'd forced me to do what I did. When I reached his door, I rang the bell. Max answered with a solemn look on his face.

"Sup?" He replied in a lowkey voice, moving aside to let me enter. When I got inside, he locked the door and set the alarm. He then walked away without saying a word. Max had always been the strong, silent type. Sometimes, getting words out of this nigga was like pullin' teeth. Whenever we hung out and went to parties, I was always the extrovert talking to everybody, while he was the introvert who preferred to stay off in the cut just observing. We were different, which is why I guess we got along good. If he didn't want to talk, I didn't push it. I always respected his space and privacy.

I reluctantly followed him to the living room, stopping at the entrance. He walked to the center of the room, folded his arms across his chest and started pacing back and forth in front of the couch. He was gathering his thoughts. The storm was brewing. I just watched him for a few seconds before I finally broke the tense silence. "Max..."

He stopped in midstride and swung around to face me. "Why you got to be so fucking hardheaded, Wicked?!" His voice boomed like thunder. "I tell you that you shouldn't do something, and you go and do the shit anyway???"

"First, you need to take that bass out your voice. Second, me and you almost the same age--stop talkin' to me like a child!"

"That's exactly how you act sometimes! Especially this sneaky shit you just pulled. I can't fucking believe you went behind my back and set up a meeting with that nigga!" He flapped his arms about as he spoke. "So what did you do—run my phone to get his number?"

"Put yourself in my shoes, man. When I realized you weren't ever gonna put me on, I did what I had to do." Realizing how defiant and unrepentant I sounded, I tried to soften my tone. "Trust me, I didn't feel good about it, but my back was against the wall and I had no other resort." I felt like I was pleading my case in a courtroom and trying to gain the jury's sympathy. Judging from the apathetic expression on Max's face, I could tell he wasn't buying my argument.

"You had other options," he countered. "Hell, I just gave you one today."

"What, AMP Records?" I asked sarcastically. "Thanks. But nah, no thanks. Believe me, man, I truly appreciate the gesture, but seriously though, why would I want to go to some second-rate label to meet with a middleman when I've already got a deal on the table at the top record label in the country? It's like you're askin' me to turn down a steak dinner at one of them expensive ass steakhouses for a fuckin' cheeseburger at McDonald's! Does that make any logical sense to you?" I threw my hands up in the air.

"Look, you don't have to go to AMP. That was only a suggestion. Like I told you over and over again, you're mad talented; if you set your mind to it, you can go to any label you want."

"Anywhere except Scorcher?" I scoffed.

"Baby, I promise, I'll do everything in my power to help you get signed somewhere besides there."

"Because for some reason, being signed to the hottest label in the industry should be off limits to me, but not to you, right? And you actually expect me to happily go along with what you want just because you say so? You must take me for a fool. Why you tryin' to play me, yo?"

"It's not even like that."

"Then what the fuck is it like??? Give me one reason, Max. Give me one good reason why I shouldn't sign!"

"Because...I love you." He walked over to me and peered into my eyes. "And I'm begging you not to."

"Oh, so I'm just supposed to walk away from this deal for love?"

"Yes. If you truly love me and care about us, you won't do it."

"So let me get this straight--you're giving me an ultimatum? You're threatening to end what we have if I don't turn this deal down?"

"I don't want you getting hurt."

"Nigga, I'm hurtin' every day without money in my pocket."

"Wicked, money isn't everything. They're more important and valuable things in this world than money."

"Like...?"

"Your soul. Your freedom. Your life."

"What do you mean? Is Scorch involved in some underhanded shit?" I probed. Max shifted his eyes, looking across the room. "Tell me, man!"

"Look, don't ask me about Scorch! I'm not talking about that nigga. I can't. If you trust me, you won't go against me on this. You just gotta believe that I have your best interest at heart. The less you know, the better off you are."

I smirked. "So ignorance is bliss, huh?"

"Yeah, in this situation, it is. I can't go into specifics, but I can tell you that Scorch isn't what he seems."

"What is he, a damn Transformer?" I mocked. It was like we were going around in circles and getting nowhere. I was tired of him being all cryptic and shit. "Okay, if the nigga is bad as you make him out to be, why the fuck are you still with him then? Why haven't you left already?"

"Believe me, I want to, but I can't." His face was dead serious. "Not yet, anyway."

"Why not? Yeah, I know you under contract and all, but if you really wanted to get out, I'm sure there's a way for you to leave."

"You don't understand. It's not that easy." He turned his back to me and exhaled a long breath. "It's...complicated." He obviously expected me to drop the subject, however, it wasn't going to happen. Not tonight. I wasn't going to stop until I got the truth out of him.

"Let me guess; he made you sign a confidentiality agreement or somethin'? The nigga got you scared to talk about him even when he's not around?" I let out a taunting laugh, attempting to get under his skin and make him crack. "Scorch got you shook like that, yo???"

He spun around with a sneer on his face. "Just shut the hell up, Wicked! You have no clue what you're talking about, so I'm not going to waste time arguing with you. I tried asking you, but you want to be hardheaded, so now I'm telling you: You might as well tear that contract up, cause there ain't no way in hell I'm letting you sign it."

Was he actually trying to "pull rank" on me? He had me fucked all the way up. "Nigga, I may've never met my daddy before, but I sure as hell no you're not him. You can't tell me what I can and can't do."

"Yeah, actually I can." He folded his arms and stared in my eyes. "One way or another, I'll see to it that it doesn't happen."

I shook my head in disbelief at what I was hearing. "You on some real powertrippin' shit right now, Max. I can't believe I've been ridin' with you all this time and never knew what type of cat you really are. Up until now, you been holdin' all the cards. Not anymore though. And that scares you, doesn't it? You can't stand the thought of me doin' shit for myself. You must be one of them dudes who love to keep bitches dependent on you to boost your ego and feed your manhood. Well, I got a newsflash for you, nigga—I'M NOT YOUR BITCH!"

"I don't think you're my bitch, but that's what you acting like right now—all in your feelings and shit!"

I'd been holding on to the tiniest sliver of hope that he had a legit reason for wanting me not to sign with Scorch. I was trying my hardest not to think the worst of him. I was now seeing him in a whole new light. This nigga was not only selfish, but also mad controlling. I felt like swingin' on his ass. "You're trying to hold me back. You just wanna keep me under your thumb and dependent on you! You like feelin' like you have control over me, huh?"

Max shook his head. "You always think you're so smart and know everything, don't you? Well, lemme tell your ass somethin--" The intercom on the wall suddenly buzzed, interrupting him. He looked at me with a leery expression. Although he seemed hesitant, he walked over and pressed the button to answer. "Yes?"

"Mr. Reeves?" Ricardo's voice squawked through the intercom speaker.

"Yeah," Max answered.

"There're two gentleman here by the name of Mr. Kane and Mr. Driggs here to see you."

Max frowned. "Alright, send them up." He scratched the back of his neck, his demeanor now noticeably anxious. "Will, I gotta handle some business right now. Please, just promise me you won't sign that contract." It seemed like his business always came before me.

"Nah, I ain't promising shit." I marched through the apartment to the front door. I heard Max's heavy footfalls behind me. He grabbed my arm.

"I'm not letting you leave this house without swearing to me you won't sign that deal."

I clenched my jaw, staring him down defiantly.

"Promise me, Will." He looked at me with pleading, almost desperate eyes.

"Fuck you."

He sighed, slowly releasing me. "Okay...I tried to warn you." He punched in the security code to disarm the alarm. He then opened the door and stood to the side. We looked at each other, not saying a word. Neither of us were going to budge. This felt like the end. He knew it and I knew; I was going to choose my career over our relationship. Fuck. Why did it have to be like this?

As I walked down the hall, I could feel his eyes still on me. I fought the urge to look back, not wanting to make this harder than it already was. I pushed the button to call an elevator, struggling to keep my emotions in check. Seconds later, the elevator doors slid open. Two goon looking niggas stepped off. One of them had dreadlocks. He mean mugged me as they passed. I got a weird vibe. There was something vaguely familiar about him. I couldn't recall where, but I knew I had seen him before. I took a step towards the elevator and paused, finally giving in to the urge to look back. The goons dapped Max up and then walked into his crib. Max had a somber look on his face. We made eye contact one last time before he disappeared inside and the door closed.

CHAPTER 6

I spent most of the next day with my son, Will Jr. When we weren't watching or talking about something Teenage Mutant Turtle-related (I swear, the boy was obsessed with that shit for some reason), we were playing video games. When dinner time came, I let him go eat in the kitchen with his grandma while I went online to research Scorcher Records and this supposed Illuminati connection Ron had been babbling about. For everything that seemed to confirm it, there were two things that debunked it. Sure, some of the artists on the roster knew people close to them who had died, but so what? Didn't we all? As far as I could tell, there was no concrete evidence that proved Scorch was the devil himself. All I saw was stupid speculation and six degrees of separation, not some secret satanic cult. A lot of the "proof" seemed to be nothin' more than misinformation and flat out bullshit. I turned my laptop off, slamming it closed. I had to meet with Scorch tomorrow to give him my decision, and here I was wasting time researching rumors and urban legends. I shook my head. I guess a part of me was desperately searching for a reason — any solid reason — not to go against Max and sign the deal. So far, I hadn't found one.

My phone's ringtone, "Ain't worried about nothin'," by French Montana started blaring. I picked it up and looked at the caller ID. *Speak of the devil*, I thought with a smirk. I accepted the call.

"Hello?"

"What you doing?" It was Max.

"I been chillin' with my son all day. I'm about to take him back to 'Nieka."

"Word? I'm in BK visiting my mom. I was just about to head home. I can come by and scoop ya'll up."

I debated it for a moment. Even though I didn't feel like seeing Max right now, I also wasn't looking forward to a long ass train ride to my baby mother's crib in Queens. "Aight."

"Cool." He sounded happy I said yes. "Be there in a minute."

About a half hour later, Max called to let me know he was outside. I hastily pulled on my coat and then helped Will into his Ninja Turtle hoody and zipped him up. When we got outside, Max's black Escalade was parked on the curb. After placing Will in the backseat, I opened the passenger side door and climbed in. I looked back at lil' Will.

"Make sure you buckle up back there, aight Donatello?"

He frowned at me and whined, "Daddy, I told you I'm Michelangelo!"

"Michelangelo, Donatello, Leonardo—what difference does it make? They're all the same—big, ugly, giant turtles." I gave him a sideways grin.

"You just mad cause I beat you in Mortal Kombat." Will snapped his seatbelt in place.

"No I ain't." I made sure the belt was secure. "And you just got lucky, Turtle Boy."

"Aye, don't go disrespecting my man like that. Call him by his name, yo."

"Thanks, Unca Max."

Maximus looked at me with a boyish smile. "No problem. Everybody knows Michelangelo is the coolest turtle." He twisted in his seat, extending a big hand to playfully mush Will's head. "Right, lil' man?"

Will giggled. "Uh, huh."

During the entire ride to Queens, we had to listen to Will's Turtle talk. Max just humored him, engaging him like he was just as excited to discuss the characters as my son. I couldn't help smiling at their interaction. They always got along well together. They adored each other. I knew I would feel bad if Max were no longer in Will's life. *Or mine.*

Once we pulled up to the curb outside the house where Tanieka lived with her mother and younger brother, I hopped out the truck and got Will out the backseat. I walked up the steps and rang the doorbell. A few seconds later, Tanieka came to the door. She looked past me and twisted her lips at the sight of Max's truck. I handed her lil' Will. She held him in her arms.

"So, have you decided what you're going to do about the contract yet?"

I shook my head no, glancing down at me feet to avoid her expected glare. "Nah...I'm still debatin'."

The harrumph sound she made told me all I needed to know. She wasn't pleased, or maybe not even surprised, that I was letting Max influence my decision. "Well, don't think too hard. Lord knows it's not like we actually *need* the money or anything--with the cost of food, clothes, daycare, health insurance, and all that other *unnecessary* stuff." The sarcasm in her tone bit me to the bone. "Anyway, you just keep on racking your brain, alright? I got to go inside and put Will to bed now so I can get some sleep myself. I have to wake up early in the morning, since I'm a *responsible* parent...unlike *some* people." Once again, she was dogging me out. If she hadn't been holding Will, I would've tore into her ass. I tried not to let her get under my skin though.

"Night, daddy," Will chirped, providing a welcome distraction from my growing anger. He had one little arm clutched around his mother's neck and used the other one to give me an enthusiastic wave.

"Night, Michelangelo, duuuddde." I leaned in and gave him a kiss on the forehead. He grimaced and vigorously wiped at the spot I'd pecked. I chuckled. "Oh, my bad. I forgot ninja turtles are too tough for that." I held out my fist to him, and he bumped it with his. "Better?"

He was all teeth. "Cowabunga!"

I smiled and looked at Tanieka. "Good night."

She rolled her eyes. "Bye, Wicked." She went inside and slammed the door behind her.

I got back in Max's truck and he pulled off. He turned to with one hand on the wheel. "So...are you comin' back to my place?"

"Should I?"

"Yeah, I want you to." He placed a hand on my thigh.

I stared out the window, still unsure of how I felt about this. I knew he was probably going to try to mend things between us in hopes of getting me not to sign the deal tomorrow. A part of me kind of hoped he could if it meant savin' our relationship. "Aight."

We drove to Manhattan in silence, apparently neither one of us knowing what to say after last night. When we arrived upstairs at his place, we just stood in the kitchen looking at each other. A few minutes of tense quietness passed before Max moved closer to me and gently caressed my face. I wanted to swat his hand away, but I didn't. The smell of the cologne I'd bought him for Christmas filled my nostrils. I loved that scent on him. He slowly leaned in to press his lips against mine. As much as I tried not to, I couldn't resist kissing him back. He gripped my hard dick through my jeans and squeezed it, causing me to moan. Why was I so fuckin' weak when it came to him? He led me back to the main bedroom. After we stripped off all our clothes, he laid me down on the bed and proceeded to eat me out so good I was practically climbing the damn bedpost. I buried my face in a pillow as he buried his tongue in my ass.

"You like that?" He asked.

"Yeah. That shit feels good, yo."

He spread my cheeks and went back to flicking his tongue against my hole. Once I was wet and open, he got out of bed to get a condom. While he was putting it on, I got on all fours. After he lubed me up, I felt the head of his hard dick push in.

I groaned and grunted, feeling him enter me. He grabbed my waist and slowly began thrusting in and out. After allowing me to get used to him inside of me, he sped his pace. "Yeah, take this ass, son."

"Throw that shit back, nigga" he ordered, slapping my ass.

I began doing as he commanded.

"You like how that dick feel?"

"Fuck yeah." I started jackin' my own dick while he plowed me hard and deep. "Damn, you hittin' that spot."

He pulled up, so my back was against his chest. His face was now next to mine.

"Take that shit," he said, thrusting into me.

"I can't take much more, yo." It was feelin' so good, I knew I was about to bust any second.

"You want this nut, Wicked?" He turned my head towards his and shoved his tongue in my mouth.

"Yeah, nigga," I said, whimpering in his mouth.

"Ah, shit…I'm cummin'!" His body shuddered. He thrust in and out a few more times causing nut to shoot out my dick onto my chest.

I slowly collapsed on the bed with him on top of me. He pulled out and rolled off of me, breathing hard. Max traced a finger along the outline of the green tattoos on my bicep. He then softly kissed the one just above my shoulder blade that said "Faith" in cursive letters. I wasn't religious or anything, but I did believe in God. I also believed if I had faith in Him, He would guide me and I would achieve my goals. No matter how hard shit got sometimes, whenever I looked at myself in the mirror, that tattoo always reminded me why I had to keep goin' and never give up on my dreams. No matter what, I had faith in God and in myself that they would eventually come to pass. And now that my prayers finally had seemed to be answered, I was seriously contemplating turning down a gift from God. And for what...?

"I love you, baby. I don't ever wanna lose you," he said. "Especially not over money."

"Max, it ain't just about the money. It's about you and me supposedly being partners, but you hidin' shit from me."

"I wish I could tell you everything, but I can't right now. All you need to know is that I have good reasons for not wanting you to sign that deal tomorrow."

"You know you're puttin' me in a tight spot, right?"

"I'm askin' you to trust me." He turned so he was facing me. "Do you?"

"Yeah…yeah I do."

I breathed a heavy sigh. "I know there're more important things in life than money, but trust and love ain't goin' to pay my bills, man. I mean, you're askin' a broke nigga to turn down guaranteed paper."

"You're not broke."

"Bruh, you haven't seen my bank account lately, have you?"

Max rolled out of bed and walked across the room. He opened a dresser drawer and pulled something out. I saw him pick up a pen and scribble something real quick. He then came back to my side of the bed and sat down. "Here," he said, handing me something. It was a check with a lot of zeroes! It was nowhere near as much as the deal Scorch had offered me, but it was still more money than I'd ever made in my life.

"Yo, what's this?" I asked in amazement.

"What's it look like?"

"Man, I can't take this." I tried to hand it back to him, but he pushed my hand away.

"Take it. That's to tide you over 'til we find you another deal."

I raised an eyebrow. "And who says I need another deal?"

He stared at me with puppy dog eyes. An uncontrollable smile slowly slid across my face.

"Aight, yo. I can't believe I'm actually goin' to turn this deal down."

Max smiled broadly and gave me an excited kiss. "You won't regret it, bae."

I took a deep breath. "Yeah, we'll see."

The following morning I walked into the offices of Scorcher Records still feelin' conflicted. I just hoped I wasn't about to throw away a once in a lifetime opportunity because I was dickmatized. I shook the thought out of my head. The reason I was about to turn the deal down was because I loved and trusted Max. Once the receptionist brought me into Scorch's office, he stood up and greeted me with a firm handshake, and then indicated for me to take a seat.

"Before we start, I just want to say something." He sat down behind his desk and tented his fingers in front of his face. "A contract is sort of like a marriage. For that marriage to work and be mutually beneficial, I believe both parties need to be forthcoming and upfront about their lives before entering into such an arrangement."

I looked at him confused. What the fuck was this dude talkin' about?

"I said all that to say, something has been brought to my attention--something I feel we need to discuss before going any further. I know we're both busy men, so I'm not about to beat around the bush--I'm just going to come right out and ask you." He leaned forward in his chair, his eyes meeting mine. "Are you gay?"

"W-what?" My stomach dropped. All of a sudden, I felt dizzy. "Hell, no. Why you ask me some shit like that?"

"Let's just say I heard it from a reliable source." He leaned back in his leather chair, keeping his scrutinizing eyes on my face.

I was flippin' out inside, my mind all over the place. Was he about to rescind his offer? Could he even legally do that? *And who the fuck could have told him about me???* "Who told you that shit, yo?" My face was tight with anger.

"Like you told me when we first spoke, that's not important. The only thing that matters is if it's true or not."

"Nah, yo. Of course it ain't fuckin' true! Do I look gay to you, son? Whoever you heard that from makin' shit up," I said confidently, hoping he couldn't tell how flustered I was. I had to fight the urge to squirm in my chair.

He didn't say anything. He just sat there staring at me as though he were waiting for me to change my response. "Okay, apparently my source got it wrong. Sorry if I offended you."

I didn't respond. I was too tight to say anything.

"Well, now that that's out the way, on to business." He steepled his fingers again and rested them against his lips. "What's the verdict?"

I pulled the paperwork from the inside pocket of my blazer and unfolded it. "I'm honored to join Scorcher Records."

A satisfied smile spread across Shameek's face. "A wise choice, Wicked." He handed me a pen.

I placed the documents on the desk and signed my name on each page he indicated. Once I was done, I slid it across the desk towards him. He picked it up and signed his own signature underneath mine, sealing the deal. He rose from behind his desk and extended a hand to me. I hastily stood up and clasped it firmly. His eyes twinkled as his smile grew wider. Shaking my hand, he said in a smooth voice, "Welcome to the family. As long as you stay loyal to me and the team, I'll always have your back. Like I said before, this is a family. Like any family, we may have disputes and disagreements, but we should never ever deal with them or discuss it outside the crew. What goes on in this camp, stays in this camp." He held on to my hand, the smile slowly vanishing from his face. "Feel me?"

"Yeah." I nodded my head. My dream had finally come true, but I wasn't happy. All I could think about was the person who tried to betray me. The person who'd gone behind my back and attempted to out me to Scorch. Max. He had to be the "reliable source" who put a bug in Scorch's ear not to sign me because I was gay. Well, his grimy plan had backfired, and I was gonna let him know face-to-face.

*****

"Man, tell me you saw that game last night!" Ricardo said when I walked into the lobby of Max's building.

"Nah, I missed it, bruh," I replied, not in the mood for our usual banter. Ricardo was around the same age as me. We would always talk about sports and pussy. (Well, actually, he did most of the pussy talk; I usually just laughed and agreed with him).

"Damn, you missed a good one." He looked at my face, studying my demeanor. I was trying not to show how pissed off I was, but like I said before, I wore my emotions on my face and my heart on my sleeve. No matter how hard I tried not to. I guess he could tell I wasn't my usual self. "You alright?"

"Yeah, I'm straight," I lied. "Just need to holla at Max right quick."

"Gotcha. He picked up the "bat phone" as we jokingly called it and pushed some buttons. "Mad Max, your boy Wicked's here to see you." He was silent for a second, then gave me the thumbs-up sign. I nodded my appreciation and made my way to the elevators. Thankfully, no old bitties got on with me. The way I was feeling at that moment, if a broad clutched her purse and gave me the screwface, I was liable to go the fuck off.

"So, how'd things going with Scorch today?" Max asked as soon as he let me in and closed the door.

"You mean before or after he asked me if I was gay?"

"What?" He seemed surprised, but he was undoubtedly faking it. "How did he know?"

"You tell me." I smirked.

"Waitaminute. You don't think I had anything to do with it, do you?"

"You the only dude I fuck with and the only one who knows about me, so what you think?" It was kind of risky for him to out me, not knowing if I'd retaliate by outing him, too, but that didn't mean shit. I remembered him telling me before we made up that he would do whatever it took to keep me from joining Scorcher. "Yo, I can't believe you were so adamant about me not signing that deal that you went behind my back and tried to sabotage my career!"

"Wicked, I would never do some shit like that. You should know better than that."

"Keepin' it real with you, I don't know what you'd do anymore, bruh. You around here keeping deep, dark secrets and shit. Who knows what all you're capable of?"

"Baby, you know me. Or at least after all these years, I hope you do. You know I'd never do anything to hurt you."

In my heart, I truly believed him. But my brain and my street smarts were screaming at me, telling me to trust no one. Ever since my first meeting with Scorch earlier in the week, there was a gnawing question in the back of my head. Until now, I wasn't going to bring it up for fear I wouldn't like the answer (if I got one). "I know you 'can't' talk about Scorch directly." I made the air quotes gesture with my fingers. "And I'll respect that. But just answer one *indirect* question for me. And if you really care about me like you say you do, you'll be 100 with me right now."

He looked at me anxiously. "Okay."

"When Scorch mentioned how he was tellin' you that he wanted to sign me...."

"Yeah...?"

"He was about to say somethin' and suddenly stopped. He said he wanted to sign me, but you told him somethin'. He seemed like he realized what he was going to say would cause some friction between us, so he caught himself." I narrowed my eyes. "What was he about to say? What did you tell him about me?"

Max lowered his head and the massaged the back of his neck with his hand in an agitated manner.

"Just be straight with me, man."

Max looked up at me, apprehensively meeting my gaze. "I told him he shouldn't sign you."

I hauled off and hit him in the face. He staggered back looking stunned. I kept coming at his ass, throwing punches. Instead of fighting back, he tried to shield himself from my blows until he managed to get close enough to wrap his arms around me and restrain me. "Lemme go so I can swing on your ass again! That way your bitch ass can run back and tell Scorch I assaulted you!" I was breathing hard, my nostrils flaring.

"Baby, I know it sounds foul, but I did it for your own good." He was struggling to hold me.

"Cut the bullshit, yo! I ain't some dumb chickenhead you can fuck over and then spit game to to make shit all better." I finally managed to push him off me. "In case you forgot, I'm Wicked. I'm always thinkin' a few steps ahead, mah nigga. I played it cool and denied that shit. He didn't reveal who told him, but he didn't have to. I figured shit out on my own. It was your ass. If you that eager to keep me from shinin', then fuck you." I reached in my coat pocket and pulled out the check he'd given me. I ripped it in half and threw it in his face. "As of today, you lookin' at the newest member of the Fiyah Spitta Camp." I opened my coat and proudly displayed the dragon medallion necklace Scorch had given me.

"You don't know what kind of situation you just got yourself into."

"Maybe not," I retorted. "But I sure as hell know what kind of shitty situation I'm gettin' myself out of."

"Will..."

"I'm done talkin', bruh. Just open the fuckin' door before I do something I won't regret."

Max just stared at me with a grim expression for a few seconds. He then exhaled and disarmed the alarm. After reluctantly opening the door, he looked at me with heavy eyes. I turned my head. I wasn't about to fall for the persuasive puppy routine again. Our personal relationship was dead. It was business only now.

"I guess we'll be seeing each other in the studio." I didn't wait for a response to my slick comment. I marched out the door, striding to the elevator. Unlike last time, the thought to look back didn't even cross my mind. I'd tried to give Max the benefit of the doubt. I was actually willing to put my trust in some nigga and possibly throw away my future based on love and blind faith. Yeah, I definitely was on some stupid shit.

Never again though.

From here on out, I was only gonna do things Wicked's way.

CHAPTER 7

We pulled up to the club surrounded by an entourage and security. When we got out of the white stretched limo, lights from cameras and cellphones started flashing. Scorch's big ass personal security guard named Byron led us to the front door where we were whisked inside. I still couldn't get over how much my life had changed in only a few weeks. It was like a hazy dream. I'd been interviewed on all the local Hip-Hop/R&B radio stations, talking about me linking up with the Fiyah Spitta Camp and Scorcher Records. Blogs were hitting me up for interviews. Even people around my way had started treating me like a celebrity, askin' for autographs and shit, and I hadn't even stepped foot in the studio yet to start working on my album. That night, Scorch was throwing a party for me at a trendy Manhattan nightclub he co-owned to celebrate my signing.

"Damn, that shit was bananas," I said, looking back in amazement at the rabid crowd on line.

"Get use to it. This is only the beginning," Scorch replied, patting me on the back.

Our whole entourage was escorted to the VIP area. Expensive bottles of chilled champagne were already set out on the tables. I felt like I was in a fucking music video. Scorch and I took a seat on one of the white leather sofas. Byron was posted at the entrance of the VIP with his arms folded, scanning the crowd with dark shades on his face like he was the Terminator.

"Some of the other members of the team will be arriving soon." Scorch poured two glasses of Cristal. "But we can go ahead and start getting turnt up." He handed me the sparkling liquid.

"That's what's up." I grinned and sipped from my glass.

Me and Scorch drank and conversed until something caught his eye. He smiled and stood up as two familiar faces made their way through the crowd surrounded by security. Byron let them into the VIP area. Scorch dapped the men up, pulling each of them into a brotherly hug.

"Wicked, I'd like you to meet your new crew."

I almost choked on my Cristal. "Oh, shit — Tommy Gunn and Harlem Hood!" I set my glass down and jumped up to dap both of them. These niggas had hip-hop on lock and were killing it in the streets. I owned all of their albums and knew practically everything about them. I ain't gonna lie, I started geekin' out like a fat fanboy at a Star Trek convention.

"What's good, fam?" Tommy Gunn said in his raspy voice. He flashed a bright smile and pulled me into a tight bro-hug. With his smooth baby face, wavy caesar, and trendy fitted clothes, he gave off a pretty boy gansta vibe. He hailed from Brick City, aka, Newark, NJ, and had been with the label for a couple of years. His rap name came from his ability to spit verses in a rapid-fire style.

"Sup?" Jaleel Rivera, aka Harlem Hood, gave me a weak handshake. A thuggish dude from the Spanish Harlem section of Manhattan, he was covered with tats and sported a perpetual five o'clock shadow. He was the first breakout star to sign with Scorcher Records.

A few minutes later, Leah Burton, more commonly known as Ms. Malicious, the First Lady of the Fiyah Spitta Camp, appeared. She was a chick from Brooklyn with an around-the-way girl appeal, however, she possessed a sick flow that put other females and even some male MC's to shame. This was one bad bitch. There were rumors floating around in the media that she and Scorch were together (or at least fucked around), but neither of them ever confirmed or denied them.

"Hello, Wicked. It's nice to finally meet you." She whipped her long, silky hair over her shoulder and extended a soft hand to me. My eyes drank her in. She was beautiful. Between these three artists, Scorcher Records had sold millions of albums.

Everyone sat down and the drinks started flowin'. We were all talking, laughing and enjoying ourselves when the music abruptly stopped. Scorch stood and faced us, still holding his glass. Someone handed him a microphone. "I'd like to make a toast." He smiled and held up his glass. "To Wicked, the newest member of the Fiyah Spitta Camp! Welcome to the family, my man!"

A round of applause went up throughout the club. All the members of my team clanked glasses with me. Scorch passed me the mic. After I said a few words of thanks and gave some shoutouts, I did a quick, impromptu freestyle performance which turnt the club even more. Looking out at the capacity crowd and seeing everyone hangin' on my every word made happy as fuck.

However, I couldn't shake the feeling that I was missing something.

Or more precisely, *someone*.

I sat down and finished the rest of my drink, then poured another one, hoping to numb the gnawing sensation I felt in my heart.

Thirty minutes later, Scorch and Ms. Malicious had wandered away from the VIP lounge to the dance floor. I was left sitting on the sofa with Hood on my left and Tommy on my right. While Hood seemed standoffish towards me, Tommy was anything but. He'd been chewing my ear off all night. The drunker he got, the more he ran his mouth. At one point, he rested his arm behind my head on the cushion.

"So, what you think of this lifestyle, bruh?"

Lifestyle? "Huh?" Was he asking what I thought he was?

"This industry lifestyle," he clarified, shouting over the music.

"Oh," I snickered. Damn, this Cris had me tipsy as a motherfucka. "It's crazy, man. I mean just a few weeks ago, I was watching you guys on TV and followin' ya'll on Twitter. Now I'm sittin' up here in VIP, surrounded by pretty bitches and poppin' bottles. Being straight up, I still feel like this is all a dream."

He laughed. "Yeah, I felt the same way at first. Lemme tell you, your life is about to totally change. It's insane at first. But after the first few months, you'll adjust. Then Scorch will drop the other shoe on you and let you know what you really signed up for."

I gave him a puzzled look. "What do you mean by that?"

"Tommy, shut the hell up, man," Hood interjected. Those were the most words he'd spoken all night. I turned to see him glaring at Tommy. "What did Scorch tell you about discussing business in public?"

Tommy's face scrunched up. "Damn, my bad, bruh. No need to get hostile and shit."

Hood shook his head. "Aye, don't listen to that nigga."

"What was he talkin' about though?"

"Nothing. He just likes to spout off at the mouth when he's fucked up." He turned his head and looked into the crowd of writhing bodies. I wanted to press the issue, but I didn't.

I could tell he was hiding something. Just like Max.

Max.

I sighed. The thought of him made my heart ache. I still couldn't believe the way things had turned out between us.

I didn't want to admit it, but I wished he was there with me. Although I'd seen him in passing a few times at the label offices, we hadn't spoken since that night when I stormed out of his place. Even though we weren't together anymore, I guess I was hoping he'd at least show up to support me on this night that meant so much to me. But nah, he was apparently still on that stupid bullshit. So fuck him.

I leaned back against the sofa and gulped my drink. By now, my head was spinning. I glanced out into the sea of people. My gaze landed on two guys standing off in the cut talking. I was only able to catch a glimpse of them in the flickering lights and smoke. I could make out dreadlocks on one of them. When the light briefly hit his face again he looked in my direction and our eyes met. I instantly knew where I recognized him from. It was the goon who'd mean mugged me a few weeks prior when I saw him getting off the elevator at Max's building. He was staring at me hard again. *Who the fuck is this dude?* I wondered, tapping Tommy on the arm.

"Yo, who is that over there?" When I turned to point him out, they were both gone.

Tommy gave me a quizzical look. "Who?"

"Nevermind." *You need to chill, Wicked*, I told myself. I was clearly buggin'. If those guys were at Max's crib and also here, that meant they obviously were down with Scorch's team. I pulled out my phone and stared at it. Why was I actually thinking about texting Max?

I suddenly noticed a sexy dark-skin chick making her way up the steps. She had on a red form-fitting dress that hugged her curves and squeezed her cleavage so tight it looked like the fabric was struggling to breathe. Byron, with his arms still folded across his chest, leaned down so she could whisper something in his ear. He nodded his head and stepped aside, allowing her entry. She oozed past him into the lounge and flashed an alluring smile. "Would you boys like a private show in the back?"

I looked at Tommy and Hood. Tommy was all teeth. Hood was still sitting there lookin' as though someone had fucked his girl and killed his kid. Did this dude ever crack a smile?

"I'm down!" Tommy said as he sprang from his chair. He grabbed an unfinished bottle from the table. "Come on, Wick. It's time for your initiation, nigga!"

"Aight." I reluctantly put my phone away and got up from the sofa. I glanced at Hood. "You comin'?"

He shook his head, sipped his drink, and scowled. "Nah, I'm good." He looked at me as if he were sizing me up. I just blew it off and followed Tommy.

"Aye, what's his problem?" I asked as we descended the steps.

"Oh, don't worry about him. He's always like that." He shrugged nonchalantly.

There was something about dude that didn't sit right with me. He seemed to have a wack, fucked up personality; totally different from his chill media persona. In spite of his rumored affiliation with a violent street gang, I'd always admired him as an artist and even owned all his CD's. But now that I'd actually met him in person, I was startin' not to feel him.

We followed the big booty chick down a narrow corridor. She led us into a dimly lit room where four topless strippers were sipping bubbly and sensually winding their naked bodies to the music. She closed the door and motioned for us to have a seat on the leather sofa. Mirrors were hung on the opposite walls.

Seconds later, a girl with exotic features approached us carrying a silver tray with some white powder and pills on it. Besides a thong and some high heels, she was butt ass naked. A beautiful smile graced her face. "Can I interest you in any party favors?"

"Nah, I'm good." I waved her off.

"Man, are you here to celebrate or what?" Tommy asked, wrapping one of his tatted arms around the girl's small waist and pulling her closer.

I laughed a little. "Yeah, but I don't fuck with coke though."

"I hear you. Try one of these then." He picked up a couple pills and handed some to me, keeping the rest for himself. "They'll get you right, mah dude!" He put one in his mouth and chugged from the Cristal, then handed the bottle to me. He looked at me expectantly.

I twisted my lips. Molly was alright, but weed was my drug of choice. I didn't want to seem like a wet blanket though. These cats obviously liked to party hard. If I was goin' to be a part of this team, I had to show them that I could hang. Hell, he was right; this was my fuckin' signing party and a nigga was gonna celebrate 'til the sun came up! I popped the molly and washed it down with the last of the champagne in my glass.

"That's what I'm talking about, yo!" He exclaimed, dapping me up. He stood up and pulled off his shirt, revealing his smooth, brown muscled chest and biceps. Homeboy's body was on point. He started dancing with two girls, one in the back and one in the front. I shook my head. This dude was out of fuckin' control.

A Puerto Rican chick with long hair and big titties glided over to me and sat on my lap. She started grinding on my dick with her back facing me. Although I didn't feel anything but annoyed, I wrapped my arms around her waist and muttered encouragements to pretend like I was enjoying it. I glanced over at Tommy. His pants were now down around his thighs. An Asian-looking chick was on her knees deepthroating his dick. From what I could see, that shit was long, thick and black. Word, Tommy definitely had a big ass gun. Just watching him aggressively grip her hair and face fuck her mouth instantly made me hard. The stripper who was giving me a lap dance reached back and gripped my dick. She turned around and gave me a smug smile as if she had something to do with it being hard. She leaned back and pressed her wet lips to my ear.

"You want me to take care of that for you, papi?"

"Nah, I'm good, ma," I said. My shit was straining against my jeans. Even though I was horny as fuck and tempted by the prospect of getting my dick wet, I didn't know where these chicks mouths had been. "I got a girl."

"Wow. About to be famous and still faithful." She smiled wistfully. "She's a lucky lady."

"That's what I be tryin' to tell her all the time." I chuckled a little. Thank God I didn't bring Tanieka. I had considered inviting her, but I didn't want any drama. Knowing her, she would've probably been up in here trying to get a comeup, and I would've had to go off on her ass. "Aye, pardon me, baby, I gotta use the bathroom right quick."

She shifted from my lap to the sofa. "Okay, I'll be here waiting."

"Cool." I had no plans on returning to this room. I stood up and adjusted my dick. I was about to mention to Tommy I was heading back to the front, but I didn't want to disturb him; he seemed lost in ecstasy while the chick was still goin' hard on his pole. I slipped out of the room and made my way through the hallway hoping I was going in the right direction.

When I entered the bathroom, it was empty. I stood at a urinal and pulled out my dick. It was still on brick. I tried to pee, but nothing came out. I kept trying to squeeze something out until I suddenly felt a pulsating sensation ripple through my body, almost as if I was about to nut. I shut my eyes and tilted my head back as I tugged at myself. That pill I'd popped had definitely kicked in. I was standing there in public at a urinal stroking my shit and not giving a fuck. I was in a euphoric zone. I felt like I was on the verge of busting one of the best nuts I'd ever had in my life until I heard someone walk in the door. *Fuck*. I opened my eyes and looked straight ahead, pretending to piss. Even though there were a bunch of empty urinals and stalls, I could feel the person stand at the urinal next to me. I didn't turn my head to see who it was, but I glimpsed him out the corner of my eye.

I was shocked when I heard him ask, "You need some help with that?"

When I looked to the side, Scorch was staring at me with a gleam in his eyes and a mischievous smirk on his face. I just stood there frozen, holding my hard dick in my hand. "W-what did you say?"

His smirk shifted into a grin. "You heard me. I never stutter."

Was this some kind of joke, or maybe even a test? "I already told you I'm not gay," I said in the most serious tone I could muster.

"Yeah, you did say that, didn't you?" His grin widened into a smile. *Is this nigga playing mind games with me???* He looked down, unzipped his pants, and pulled out his dick. I couldn't help noticing he was hard. His shit was a shade darker than he was, thick and slightly curved to the left. "But we both know that's a lie." His voice was so sure, so confidant. He suddenly turned and looked dead in my face.

"Man, w-what--" I was stammering and sputtering like a lame. *Shit! He caught me checking him out.* He extended a hand towards my dick, pushing mine out the way. I tried to weakly protest. "Nah, bruh. What the fuck you…"

"Relax." He licked his pink lips. "I got you."

I just stood there as his fingers firmly wrapped around my hard shaft, still not believing this was actually happening. With the molly and alcohol flowing through my system, everything seemed surreal. It was like a dream. A crazy ass wet dream. The owner of the hottest hip-hop record label in the world was about to give me a fucking handjob in a club bathroom.

Oh shit!

Remembering where we were, my eyes widened in panic. "What if someone comes in here?"

"They won't." There was that confidant tone again. He seemed so sure of himself, so in control of everything. He held my gaze, his grey eyes seemingly entrancing me. He started stroking me, his fist sliding up and down the length of my dick, sending waves of intense pleasure through my entire body.

I gasped and let out a low moan. My senses felt heightened. I'd never felt so in tune with my body before. My heart was beating faster. My breaths coming quicker. God, this felt so fucking amazin'. But why was I feeling so conflicted? I wanted to come, but I couldn't. What if this was some kind of setup? *If I came, that would be all the proof he needs that I'm gay.* All kinds of stupid, paranoid shit like that was rushing through my mind. I began to panic.

"Just let go," Scorch commanded in a calm, yet firm voice. I glanced down to see him jerking his dick in unison with mine. He seductively bit his bottom lip, those penetrating eyes of his burrowing into my psyche. "You're good. I got you."

That bit of reassurance was apparently all my subconscious mind needed to hear. I shut my eyes and sucked in a breath. A warm sensation washed over me. My dick throbbed and pulsed. I felt the cum shoot out of me so hard my knees almost gave way. I fell forward a little, placing a hand against the wall to steady myself.

"That's what's up," I heard Scorch say. He started jacking his own dick with the hand he'd just gotten me off with, using my cum as lube. He was beating his shit hard and fast. All I heard was a wet, fapping sound. It didn't take long before he tilted his head back and grunted, his shoulders shuddering. We stood there in silence, both of us breathing hard. Without saying a word, Scorch walked over to the sinks and turned on the water. I hesitantly joined him in front of the mirrors, lathering and washing my hands.

I felt hella awkward. Why wasn't he talking? Was I supposed to say somethin' first? What the fuck do you possibly say after your new boss just gives you a fuckin' handjob? I stole a glance at his reflection in the mirror and quickly looked away, pretending to be extra focused on getting my own hands clean. Why was he casually carrying on as if nothin' had even happened???

After he finished, he grabbed some paper towels from the dispenser and dried off, then tossed them away. I did the same. I nervously glanced at him out the corner of my eye to see him briefly run a hand through his curly hair and give himself a once-over in the mirror.

His eyes glanced downward to his right. "Fix your pants."

I looked down and hastily pulled up my zipper, the back of my neck heating in embarrassment. "Uh, thanks, yo."

He nodded his head and then walked away. I exhaled a soft breath and followed suit, still not sure what had just happened. Hell, maybe I'd been hallucinating? Who knows what was in that shit Tommy gave me? I heard Scorch knock on the door. A second later, it opened and I followed him out the restroom. Byron and two equally huge security guards were in the hall. A few niggas were standing in line, some looking annoyed and some anxious, obviously because they were barred from entering while me and Scorch were in there. They quickly rushed in as we passed, Byron leading us through the hallway as if he was escorting the president and shit. When we got back to the party, it was still going strong. The DJ was blasting tracks from The Fiyah Spitta Camp and the crowd seemed like it'd gotten even larger. As we pushed our way through, bitches were trying to grab me and niggas tried to give me pounds. Our mini-army of guards shut them down though, pushing and shoving people like it wasn't nothin'.

Once we were finally within a few feet of the VIP section, I saw him. My heart stopped. Max turned his head and looked in our direction from where he was sitting, talking to Hood. He kept his gaze trained on us as we ascended the steps and approached him. Malicious and Tommy had returned also.

"Mr. Maximus, you made it!" Scorch leaned in and gave him a half-hug.

"Yeah, sorry I'm late," he said half-heartedly. "Got hung up with something."

"Yo, Max, in case you don't know," Tommy started to say, jumping up and placing a hand on my shoulder, "this right here is--"

"I know who he is," Max said drily. "We already met."

"You have?" Tommy sounded confused.

"Yeah…a few days before I got signed." I couldn't even look at Max. My emotions were all over the fuckin' place. It was like anger, guilt, happiness and sadness were all battle rappin' inside me for supremacy.

"Oh, aight." Tommy sat back down, grabbed another bottle from the table and popped it open. "Anybody want some of this?" Before anyone had a chance to reply, he took it to the head and started chugging it down.

Ms. Malicious gave him the side-eye and shook her head, holding up her empty glass. "Damn, nigga."

Tommy lowered the bottle and wiped his mouth with the back of his hand. He looked at her with an oblivious expression on his face. "What?"

She rolled her eyes and then daintily crossed her bare legs, putting on a smile. "So, are you enjoying yourself, Wicked?"

"Uh, yeah." I tried to hide my nervousness and inner turmoil as I found a place on the circular sofa. "This shit is fiyah."

"This is how we do it over here," Scorch said, sitting next to me and draping an arm on the cushion behind my head. "We work hard, and party harder. Now that you've got the party part out the way, it's time to get to work." He chuckled a little. "We're going to get you in the studio this week. You ready?"

"Hell yeah!" Regardless of how it happened, finally getting in a recording studio to begin working on my album was one thing I had no conflicting emotions about. "I can't wait to get in that booth!"

Scorch smiled. "I'm eager to hear what you and Max come up with when you get alone."

"No doubt." My mood dampened a little at the prospect of working with Max. I knew I would have to, but it wasn't something I was looking forward to. I tried to fake enthusiasm. "I know whatever we come up with is gonna be hot, yo!"

Max smirked and took a sip from his glass. I quickly averted my eyes and looked at my wristwatch, suddenly feeling ready to go.

We stayed a little longer, talking and drinking until it was almost closing time. The entire entourage left the VIP and walked to the exit doors. As soon as we got outside, a line of chauffeured Escalades pulled up to the curb. Tommy dapped off with everyone before staggering into one of the trucks with two women on his arm. I guess he was planning on having an after party.

Scorch dapped off with the remaining crew members and then addressed me. "One of these rides will take you home. Just let the driver know if you want him to stop somewhere and get breakfast or something. It won't be long before you'll have a place here in Manhattan like the rest of the crew so you won't have to travel all the way to BK." He smiled and pulled me into a brotherly hug. "Once again, welcome to the family, my man. Trust me, this is just the start of a long, prosperous and mutually beneficial relationship." He leaned in close, his lips brushing against my ear as he whispered, "In more ways than one." My blood ran cold. When he pulled away, he had a sly grin on his face.

"Nice meeting you, Wicked." Ms. Malicious said in an overly sweet voice. She smiled and batted her fake eyelashes. Even though she had money, you could tell she was still a hood chick trying to put on an air of sophistication. Byron opened the door so she and Scorch could climb in. He and another guard then got in.

I stood there dumbfounded as I watched them speed away. What had happened between me and Scorch tonight, and what the hell did it mean for my future?

"Congratulations," Max said, resting a hand on my shoulder and snapping me out of my daze. "You made it to the *big times*, mah dude." He sounded sincere, but there was also a hint of sarcasm in his voice.

"Yeah, no thanks to you." I glared at him expecting to see a smug expression. Instead, his face was stoic, almost melancholy. Did he possibly know about what me and Scorch had done in the bathroom?

"Enjoy it while you can...cause it's not going to last long. You'll soon find out just how dysfunctional your new 'family' really is." Before I could reply, he walked off and got in the back of an awaiting Escalade where Harlem Hood was already seated. The truck pulled off, leaving me with more questions and no answers in sight.

CHAPTER 8
MAXIMUS

I stared at Wicked from the window as we drove past him. Why did he have to be so fucking hardheaded???

"You sure your manz can be trusted?" Hood asked me.

"I told you, he's cool."

"Ight...I'll take your word for it." He didn't seem convinced. "I can't wait 'til we take that nigga Scorch out, yo."

"Yeah, I feel you," I replied grimly. If Scorch knew we were plotting on him, both of our lives would be forfeit. If they weren't already.

This wasn't supposed to happen. I loved Will. I'd gone out of my way to protect him, but it seemed to be all in vain now. It was like everything had blown up in my face. As hard as I'd tried to shield him from this craziness, I still failed. Now that he was unexpectedly in the mix, things were even more complicated and urgent than before. I felt as though I was attempting a dangerous stunt, like walking a tightrope between skyscrapers with no safety net. *How is all of this going to play out?* I wondered, vacantly staring out the window as the Escalade drove me home.

Home.

It wasn't too long ago that merely the thought of calling a luxury apartment in an upscale building on the Upper Eastside put an uncontrollable smile on my face. I still remembered the first day I brought Wicked to my new crib. I was so happy and excited I actually tongued him down in the elevator ride up to my floor. It seemed like all my hard work and perseverance was finally beginning to pay off. I would now be able to provide for my baby girl, my family and loved ones, while doing what I loved. I was actually living my dream, and I couldn't wait for Will to share it with me.

Until several months ago, when Scorch turned it into a nightmare.

I shifted in the bucket seat and placed a hand over my face, massaging my throbbing temples. Just the act of recalling the night everything changed gave me a headache.

My adrenaline started pumping the same way it had that night.

The Fiyah Spitta Camp had gathered at one of Scorch's many cribs. It was there that he dropped an atomic bomb on me.

"Nigga, this is supposed to be a music company," I'd snapped. "That's what the fuck it said on the contract I signed. You can keep all this extra shit!"

He chuckled. "Max, my man, don't be so naïve and myopic. We're all business people in this room; as such, we always have to look at the big picture. And the bottom line for any serious businessman is getting the almighty dollar…any and every way possible."

I shook my head at him in disgust before turning my attention to Tommy Gunn, Harlem Hood, and Ms. Malicious, who were sitting on the sofa looking unbothered. "And you all are cool with this?"

Tommy took a pull of the blunt he was holding and shrugged his shoulders. "It is what is." He passed it to Ms. Malicious. She put it to her pouty lips and pulled, casually crossing her legs like she was Sharon Stone in that movie "Basic Instinct."

Hood just folded his arms over his chest and gave me an apathetic smirk.

I shouldn't have been surprised that they would be down with this insanity. They were hood niggas who would do anything for a dollar long before Scorch signed them. Just because they now lived in lavish homes and pushed expensive cars, that didn't change their street mentality. They had no qualms about doing any and everything to get paper. To an extent, Will was the same way. Although I loved him, that was one of the few things I hated about him.

"See, everybody's onboard with the family business, man."

"Yeah, well I'm not. I want out of my contract, Scorch."

"Too bad, because I'm not letting you out."

"Well, I'm breaking that shit then."

"I highly doubt that. It wouldn't be beneficial for you in any way to do so. If you try to break it, you'll more than likely end up broken."

I stared him up and down with a scowl. Scorch had a nice build on him, but I was confident I could drop his pretty ass if I had to. "You think you can intimidate me to make me go along with this?"

"I don't like the word 'intimidate'. I never force anyone into anything. I'd rather persuade than intimidate. You're a smart dude. I think you can be convinced to see things my way." He rested a hand on my shoulder. I snatched it off.

"Keep on thinking that, bruh. You can threaten to sue me twenty ways from Sunday-- that's not gonna keep me in your camp."

"Who said anything about suing you?" He had a blithe smile on his face. "I have less costly and significantly less troublesome ways of getting what I want." His smug, cocky demeanor pissed me off.

"Talk all the shit you want. If I go public with this, you'll have a big problem on your fucking hands. You and your label would be finished."

"Perhaps." His expression turned serious. "But then again, I have ways of making problems and the people who create them go away. Permanently."

"Are you threatening me? I'm not afraid of you." I was seconds away from yoking him up and kicking his ass.

He raised a hand and snapped his fingers. Byron stepped forward and pulled his blazer back a little to reveal the handle of a gun in his waistband.

When I looked into Scorch's icy eyes, it was clear he wasn't bluffing. He was dead serious. This man was dangerous. The fight slowly left me.

"So, are you still down with the Fiyah Spitta Family?"

I reluctantly met his gaze, trying to conceal my contempt. "Yeah…I'm down."

"Max, we're here." Hood's voice snapped me out of my memories. Not long after that night, he'd approached me in secret and revealed he also wanted out of his contract.

"Good looking out. I'll get at you later."

"Aight. Stay up. Like I said, I gotta strange feeling Scorch may be on to us."

I nodded my head and dapped off with him. I opened the door to get out. I didn't want a personal driver or a bunch of security like Scorch and the rest of them. I wasn't immersed in that world or about that life. Or at least I didn't want to be anyway. All I ever wanted to do was make music. However, being trapped at Scorcher Records had slowly chipped away at that creative passion, as well as my happiness. I sighed as I closed the door and watched the truck drive off. Hopefully, it wouldn't be long until I was free.

"Maxwell." His voice made my skin crawl. I turned to my left to see Driggs seemingly appear out of nowhere. As usual, there was a lit cigarette hanging from his mouth.

"Damn, you gotta follow me around everywhere?" I glared at him. He had a bad habit of popping up unannounced, just as he'd done that day when Wicked was at my place.

"Just doing my job, boss."

Boss. I hated when he called me that. There was always an undercurrent of derisiveness behind it. I knew he only called me that and referred to me by my real name just to be a dick.

"That was a nice 'lil party. Your boy looked like he was having a good time in the VIP poppin' bottles."

"Yeah," I said frowning, "for now."

He removed the cigarette from his lips and narrowed his eyes at me . "You sure he doesn't already know what's up?"

"Nah, I told you before that he's not involved in that. He signed on with them only a few weeks ago. Trust me, he doesn't know anything." Even though Will had gone behind my back to sign with Scorch, I was still trying to protect him and keep him off the radar (which is also why I'd attempted to keep everything a secret up until now).

"If you say so," he replied, sounding doubtful. He took a puff of his cigarette and exhaled the smoke.

I fanned a hand in front of my face and shot him an irritated look. I hated cigarette smoke. "How much longer is all of this gonna take?" I'd made a deal with the devil by signing with Scorch. And now, to regain my freedom, I was possibly dealing with an even worse devil.

"Not long now, boss." He tossed the rest of the cig on the ground and snuffed it out with his Timberland. "Just make sure you remember our arrangement, and keep your mouth shut. We don't want anyone getting wind of what's about to happen."

"Yeah, tell me something I don't know." I couldn't stand this dude. "Anything else?"

"Nope." He turned and began to walk away, his dreadlocks hanging down his back. "Enjoy the rest of your night, boss."

I watched him disappear into the night before going inside. I knew this was a dangerous game I was playing, but my back was against the wall and I had no other way out. Everything had already been set in motion, and the dominoes were about to start falling. I just prayed I'd be able to get Wicked out the way before the shit hit the fan.

CHAPTER 9

I lived by a set of self-imposed rules. Or, at least I tried to anyway. Those rules weren't written in stone, and could be bent when and if the need arose. However, there were things even I wouldn't do, certain lines I wouldn't cross. My two main no-no's were: I didn't steal, and I didn't kill.

Yeah, I may've sold a little weed, but, I'd never sold "real" drugs. I wasn't out there slingin' crack or other poisonous shit. I also wasn't out there robbing and shooting at people indiscriminately and hittin' incident bystanders, or beefing with niggas over gang rivalries, blocks, or other stupid shit. I had hustled on the streets because I needed to survive and live somehow, but I always knew it was only temporary. When the opportunity came to better myself so I could provide for my son and give him a financially secure future, I seized it.

So far, I had no regrets.

That's what I kept tellin' myself as I stood in the recording booth, peering at Max and Scorch in the control room through the glass. However, after what had gone down the night before at the club, seeing them sitting next to each other listening to me while I rapped into the mic was hella awkward and mentally jarring. Scorch was acting as if the whole bathroom incident at the club hadn't happened, so I was just going to do the same thing. I felt a little bad about it once the high wore off, but I tried to push those guilty thoughts out of my mind. After all, I reasoned, it wasn't like Max and I were still together...*or would ever be again*. It took everything in me to focus and remember what this whole rap thing was really all about for me: 'lil Will. Keeping him in mind helped me get my head straight and focus on the task at hand.

After a rough start and a few takes, I finally got into my groove and started flowin' over Max's hot track like melted butter. Scorch bobbed his head and smiled, giving me the thumbs up sign. I was happy to see him pleased with what he was hearing. Once I came to the end of the song we were working on, Scorch held up his hand and motioned for me to come out. I removed my headphones and joined them in the control room.

"We've had a productive day, fellas," Scorch said, clapping. He pushed away from the soundboard and turned in his chair to face me. "Wicked, you need to go home and get some sleep. I want you well rested; you've got a big day ahead of you tomorrow."

"Word?" I furrowed my brow. "Why?"

"Malicious has a video shoot in Miami in the morning. I want you and some of the other crew members to be in it."

"Really?" I asked excitedly. I couldn't believe this shit! "I'm gonna be in a music video???"

Scorch smiled. "It's only a cameo appearance, but it'll be good exposure for you."

"Yeah, no doubt." I was all smiles as I rubbed my palms together in anticipation. I glanced over to see Max frowning. Why wasn't I surprised?

"You sure you can't come?" Scorch looked over his shoulder at Max.

"Nah, unfortunately not. I have some family business to take care of."

"I got you. Family comes first. How's your little girl, by the way?"

"She's doing good." Max averted his eyes to the control panel and toyed with a switch.

Scorch smiled. "How's she adjusting to life outside of New York?"

"Fine. She likes it in the ATL." Max had moved his baby momz and little girl down south a month ago. *But he told me they went to Florida.* Why the hell would he lie about that? Was homeboy a fucking pathological liar? Could anything he said be trusted anymore?

We spent a few more minutes wrapping up the session. It had been a long ass day in the studio, and I was hungry and mad tired. After dapping off with Scorch and Max, I made my way to the restroom. I pissed and then washed my hands. As I held them under the hand dryer, I heard the door open. I turned to see Max approaching me with a serious face. Shit, these niggas stayed runnin' up on me in the bathroom.

"Will, we need to talk."

"About what...?" I asked with attitude in my voice.

"You can't get on that plane tomorrow."

"Oh, yeah? Just watch me, yo."

He looked around, all paranoid, making sure we were alone. When he spoke, his voice was barely above a whisper. "Some serious illegal shit goes on behind the scenes here."

My eyebrow went up. "Like what?"

"Shit that can land you behind bars for a long time if you get mixed up in it."

I gave him an incredulous look. Was this a fuckin' joke? "*If* that's true, why couldn't you have just told me this before?"

"Believe me, I wanted to tell you everything, but I had to keep you in the dark for your own safety. Or...at least I was *trying* to keep you in the dark." He gave me a subtle smirk. "For all the good it did, since you just went behind my back anyway."

"I'm not even tryin' to hear your bullshit right now, Max. What's done is done. If you got somethin' to tell me, then man the fuck up and say it. Otherwise, my black ass is gonna be down in Miami." I started to walk away.

"Listen to me," he said through gritted teeth, grabbing my arm. "We can't talk right now, but I'll tell you everything later tonight. I promise. Just don't get on that plane with him in the morning." There was a sense of urgency in his tone.

"And what the fuck am I supposed to say? I already told him I'd go? Even if I wanted to, how am I supposed to back out now?"

"Lie. Make some shit up. Tell him you have an emergency or somethin'."

"Why should I do that?"

"You said you trusted me before, right?"

"Yeah...but that was before I found out you tried to out me to Scorch."

"I already told you I didn't have anything to do with that. You know I would never do anything to intentionally hurt you like that."

I remained silent, attempting to search his eyes for sincerity. At this point, I honestly didn't know if I could believe a word he was saying.

Just then, someone walked in the door. Max quickly released his grip on my arm and tried to act normal. Scorch's security guard, Byron, nodded his head at us on the way to the stalls.

Max stared at me peculiarly. "But like I was saying--you murdered that track, mah dude."

"Uh, yeah, I had to, yo." I glanced at the stall Byron had gone into. I didn't know what the hell was going on, but I just followed Max's lead and played it cool. "That beat was sick! I ain't have no choice but to kill it in a Wicked way."

We pretended to wash our hands, trading awkward looks in the mirror. After drying off, we exited the restroom together. We walked a few feet down the hall before Max stopped me.

He waited until two people went by before leaning in close and speaking in a hushed tone. "I know I've been acting all weird and secretive lately, but I promise you, there's a good reason for it. Everything is going to make sense once I explain. I'll come by your place around eight, OK?

I twisted my lips. Although he seemed genuine about finally being one hundred with me, I wasn't going to pass up an opportunity for national exposure based on bullshit innuendos. He had ample time to tell me the truth before I signed with the label, but he never would. Why the fuck should I even bother listening to him now? And who's to say if I did that he wouldn't just try to feed me more lies?

"Will...please." He stared into my eyes.

"Alright. Eight on the dot," I said firmly. I still had my reservations about trusting anything he said, but I reluctantly agreed to hear him out. This was his last chance.

*****

I looked at my phone for the umpteenth time before tossing it aside in anger. It was nine o'clock and Max hadn't shown, called or texted. I'd called him at 8:30pm, but it had gone to voicemail. What kind of stunt was he pulling? He seemed mad tense when we spoke earlier in the restroom. Maybe he'd partied too hard with that nigga Tommy Gunn and his brain was fucked up now or somethin'?

My phone's ringtone started blaring.

"Damn, about time," I mumbled, still pissed but feeling a little relieved Max hadn't completely flaked out on me. I reached over and picked it up. It was Scorch. I wondered what he could want at this time of night. "Hello?"

"Wicked, my man, what's good?"

"Ain't nothin'. Chillin'. Sup?"

"Where are you?"

"Uh, home…?"

"Get dressed."

"Why?"

"We're flying out in an hour."

"What? Are you serious?"

"Yes. There've been some scheduling conflicts, and we need to be on the set of the video earlier than expected."

"Uh…." This video cameo would be a major step in my career. Why the fuck was I hesitating?

"I'll have my driver come get you in thirty minutes. Cool?"

I thought about what Max had said about not getting on the plane with Scorch. Then I thought about how he'd stood me up. *Fuck that nigga.* I was tired of all the mind games and manipulation. He'd played me for the last time.

"Okay…I'll be ready."

CHAPTER 10

When we got off the private plane, two black Escalades were already waiting for us. Byron opened the door to one of them and me and Scorch climbed in the back. As Byron closed the door and went around to get in the passenger seat up front, I noticed dudes unloading some duffel bags from the plane into the second Escalade.

"I was in such a rush, I didn't even have a chance to pack anything to wear. Looks like you got me covered though," I said grinning.

"Huh?" Scorch gave me a puzzled look.

"All those duffel bags they unloaded off the plane." I motioned with my head toward the window. "Clothes, right?"

"Oh." Scorch chuckled. "No." I expected him to tell me what was in them, but he didn't. "They'll be wardrobe on the set."

"Aight, cool." I looked out the window as we rode through the streets of Miami. The architecture, the colorful neon lights on the buildings, the palm-tree lined streets — it was all so vibrant, so different from New York. As we drove across a long bridge the light from the moon reflected in the shimmering body of water beneath us. The whole scene was breathtaking.

We soon pulled up to a two-story white, waterfront mansion illuminated by bright lights and surrounded by palm trees. There was also a multi-car garage and cascading water at the entrance of the house.

"This is the mansion for the video shoot?" I asked, my eyes all wide and shit.

"Yep. It's also where we're staying for the night."

"Word?" I asked excitedly.

"Why should we stay in a five-star hotel when I'm already renting a mansion? The production team will be here first thing in the morning to set up for the video."

Once we got inside, Scorch gave me a tour of the house. My mouth was open the entire time. There were stainless steel appliances, onyx countertops, vaulted ceilings, and marble and hardwood floors throughout. This shit had to cost a guap.

"This place has six bedrooms and seven baths. It also has a gourmet kitchen, gym, elevator, separate guest quarters, courtyard gardens, and heated pool," he said, sounding like a realtor.

I looked around in awe. "Damn, this crib is sick."

"It's nice, but I've seen better," he replied casually.

"Yeah, I bet you have. Must be nice to have it like that." I followed him up a winding staircase.

"Trust me, my man; just do what I say and you'll be living the same way in no time." He put an arm around my shoulder. "Private jets, chauffeured cars, beautiful girls and good-looking guys — everything will soon be at your fingertips."

I felt uneasy at his mention of "good-looking guys". I glanced down over the balcony at Byron who was standing below, now talking on his cellphone. I wondered if he or anyone else had heard Scorch. Come to think of it, the place seemed eerily quiet. "Where's the rest of the crew?"

"Still flying in or already at hotels."

"So we're the only ones staying here tonight?"

He nodded his head, biting his bottom lip. "Anything wrong with that?"

"What about....?"

"Byron?"

"Yeah."

"He's my right hand man; been with me from the very beginning. There's nothing he doesn't already know about me."

"So, you trust him to keep your business secret?"

"Yes, even though I can tell he gets sick of the way I boss him around sometimes." He smiled a little. "He's not going anywhere or saying anything."

"How can you be so sure?"

"He knows better." He was serious again.

"I see." I didn't know how I felt about this. He'd obviously flown us here early to give himself an opportunity to push up on me. Scorch was a handsome dude and all, but that didn't mean I wanted to do anything with him. Sure, I'd let him give me a handjob before, but that was when I was high and shit. Now that I was sober, things were different.

When we got back downstairs, we wound up in the living room. There was a gigantic flat screen TV mounted on the wall. We sat down on a leather sectional sofa. Scorch grabbed the remote from the glass table and clicked it on. A few minutes later, Byron entered the room carrying a chilled bottle of champagne and two glasses. He handed me and Scorch each a glass and then popped open the bottle.

"Thanks, my man," Scorch said as Byron filled his glass. He then filled mine to the rim.

"'Preciate it, bruh," I said. When Byron left the room, I leaned over to Scorch and asked, "Maybe Byron can join us for a drink?"

He shook his head, chuckling. "He knows his place."

I just sipped from my glass without responding. If I didn't know any better, I would've sworn he thought Byron was his butler or something.

For the next thirty minutes, we talked with the television playing in the background. Byron had disappeared to another area of the sprawling house and hadn't returned since. In between refills, Scorch and I discussed the concept for the video being shot in the morning. The more we drank, the more buzzed I felt. I started zoning out without even realizing it until I heard Scorch's voice.

"Is something wrong?"

"Wha?"

"You look like something's on your mind."

"Oh. Yeah. Kinda." I'd been lost in thought, mostly over Max. I wondered why he'd stood me up, why he hadn't bothered to return my call, and what he'd meant when he said there was some "serious illegal shit" going on at Scorcher Records.

"What's up?" He leaned forward, looking me in the eye. This was my opportunity to find out once and for all.

"Are you involved in other business besides music?"

He smiled. "Of course I am. I'm an entrepreneur, I have my fingers in all sorts of businesses."

"I'm talking about illegal stuff, man."

"Where did you hear that from?" His forehead crinkled.

"I got my ways." I kept my eyes on him, studying his reaction. "So, you didn't deny it; is it true?"

He set his glass down on the table. "I don't usually discuss this until later, but I already feel I can trust you to keep secrets." He smiled flirtatiously and rested a hand on my thigh. "Cross country tours, coast-to-coast business-related travel—being in the music industry provides the perfect front for inconspicuously transporting certain goods across state lines." He gave me a knowing look. My heart started beating fast as I read between the lines. Was he actually saying what I thought he was? This was what Max had tried to warn me about. This was why he didn't want me getting mixed up with him. Scorch had phrased it in fancy terms, but when you cut to the chase, he was telling me that his record label was a cover for drug trafficking!

"So basically, the artists who work for you are nothin' but glorified drug mules?"

"Of course not." He appeared offended. "I like to think of you as my partners in a diversified enterprise." This nigga knew he could sugarcoat shit.

"This is crazy, yo!" I stood and paced the length of the living room floor. "I signed with you to make music, that's it."

"And that's exactly what you will be doing. The drug game is only a small part of what we do--a side business, if you will." He rose from the sofa and approached me.

I couldn't believe how nonchalant he was being. This nigga was talking about operating a drug trafficking ring as though it were nothing more than a lemonade stand. "I don't get it--you've sold hundreds of thousands of albums—why do you need to be involved in illegal side shit, too?"

"Wicked, my man, the drug game is what brought us this far. We wouldn't even be standing here without it. Where do you think I got the financial backing to start my own label — a small business loan?" He let out a snide laugh. "Just because I've been successful in my music endeavors doesn't mean I can now turn my back on those who helped me get here. It doesn't work like that. Favors have to be returned, and debts must be repaid. There's a price to pay for everything."

There's a price to pay for everything.

Those words echoed in my head. I remembered Max had said the same thing to me. Now I fully understood what he meant. "I'm sorry, Scorch, but I'm not cool with this. I have a kid and shit to think about. I'm not gonna risk goin' to prison and not being in his life because I got caught up in some bullshit I had no idea was even goin' on."

"Will, no one's going to prison. Look, it's not like I'm asking you to personally sell it; we have street teams who handle that."

"It doesn't matter if I'm sellin' it or not, I still know about it—which makes me a fuckin' accessory if something goes down." I shook my head. "I don't think I want anything to do with this label anymore, yo."

"Like I told you before you signed the deal; this is a family." He stroked his chin with his hand. "And this is one family you can't disown. You're too talented to let go of, Wicked. I'm not going to let you make the mistake of walking away from what promises to be a mutually beneficial relationship. If you know what's good for you, you'll just focus on making your album and act like this conversation never happened."

I stared him up and down like he was crazy. "You think you can bully me to make me stay and not say anything to anyone about this?"

"I don't 'bully' people. I never force anyone into anything. I believe I can persuade anyone to do what I want, especially when not doing so would go against your financial and personal self-interests."

I smirked. "So you said all of that to say you're gonna sue me if I leave, right?"

"No, I wouldn't do anything like that." A sinister smile appeared on his face. "I hate resolving disagreements in the courts. It's so time consuming. I prefer to handle my disputes in less costly and significantly less troublesome ways." He was so damn smug and arrogant.

"Are you threatening me?" I squared up with him. "I ain't scared of you, son."

"You should be. You have no idea what I can do to you…or the people you care about."

My blood ran cold. When I looked into Scorch's grayish eyes, it was clear he wasn't bluffing. He was dead serious. This nigga was actually threatening my family. Without even thinking, I punched him in the face. He fell to the floor and I jumped on his ass. He screamed for Byron like a bitch, but I just kept swinging. Suddenly, a pair of big hands yanked me off of him and slung me across the floor. I looked up to see Byron standing over me with a gun pointed at my head. Scorch got to one knee, rose to his feet, and then walked over to me.

"Don't ever put your fucking hands on me," he said through clenched teeth. He kicked me in the gut twice with his shiny, hard toe shoe. "You hear me?!" He sneered, his face contorted and his eyes wild. The cool, calm and collected veneer had been peeled away. The professional "businessman" was gone. I was now seeing another side to Scorch. The real side. "I said, DO YOU HEAR ME?!"

I curled up in the fetal position, clutching my stomach in pain. I glared at him, slowly nodding my head.

He seemed satisfied with my response. Once he regained his composure he asked in a smooth voice, "Are you still down with the Fiyah Spitta Family?"

I knew going against him right now would get me hurt, or possibly worse. "Yeah...."

"Good." He started unbuttoning his shirt. "Now, stand up and take those clothes off."

CHAPTER 11

My face twisted. "What?"

He opened his shirt to reveal a smooth, muscular chest and a chiseled six-pack. "You heard me. I want to find out how that sexy ass of yours feels around my dick."

"Nigga, I told you before that I don't get down like that," I said, scowling.

Scorch smirked. "That's why you let me have my way with you in the bathroom?"

"I was fucked up; it was a one-time thing."

"Sure it was." His lips spread into a devilish grin. "I guess only Max gets to hit it, huh?"

"W-what the fuck are you talkin' about?" I tried to play it off, but he obviously could tell by my reaction that I was shook by what he'd said.

"Yes, I know about you two." The smile disappeared from his face. "I know everything."

"I don't know what the hell you're talkin' about, or what you may think you know, but I'm still not lettin' you fuck me."

"It's okay. You'll come around soon and give it up. But in the meantime," he unzipped his pants, "some head will suffice." He pulled his dick out of his pants and just let it hang. Although it was soft, it was long and thick. He took hold of it and began stroking it. Once it grew to its full length and hardness, he smacked it against my cheek and then smeared it across my lips. I didn't move or breathe. "Open your mouth."

I stared up at him defiantly.

"I said, OPEN YOUR FUCKING MOUTH!"

I clenched my jaw tighter and glared at him.

"I see you need some persuading." He glanced at Byron, who took that as the cue to step closer and shove his gun in my face. He pressed the cold steel barrel against my lips. My heart pounded in my chest. "You can either have that in your mouth, or my dick...the choice is yours. I'd hate for you to go M.I.A. in MIA."

I reluctantly swallowed my pride and slowly opened my mouth.

"That's more like it." Scorch had a smug grin on his face. Byron moved to the side, putting the barrel of the gun to my temple. Scorch placed the brown mushroom head of his dick to my lips and pushed it into my mouth. I could taste the saltiness of his precum. He gripped my head in his hands and began fucking my face like it was a pussy, his big dick thrusting in and out of my mouth. He hit the back of my throat a few times, causing me to gag. That didn't stop him though; he just kept bucking his hips.

After a few minutes of him controlling the situation, I decided to take charge. I began aggressively sucking and jerking him off at the same time. I just wanted to make him cum and get this over with. Even though the television was on, the only things I could hear were loud slurping sounds and my heart pounding in my ears. Saliva was running down the corners of my mouth and my neck was hurting, but I kept on sucking him off like my name was Superhead.

"Yeah, suck that dick." He closed his eyes and tilted his head back, letting his mouth hang open. His ab muscles flexed with each breath he took. He was close. I could feel his already hard dick stiffen even more. He clasped my head with his hands and grunted. With one last pump, I felt his dick spasm, filling my mouth with warm, salty cum. He kept his throbbing dick in my mouth for a few minutes, letting it soften before putting it back in his pants.

I spat his nut on the floor in disgust and wiped my mouth with the back of my hand.

"Damn, you give good head for a 'straight' nigga. I'd love to sample that ass of yours tonight, but I can wait…for now. " He looked at me with a cocky grin.

I just glared at him with hatred burning in my eyes.

This nigga was going to pay for violating me.

*****

"Wicked, try to look like you're having fun!" The director yelled as he broke from filming.

We were shooting a poolside scene for Malicious' music video. Me and the other members of the Fiyah Spitta Camp were surrounded and being groped by bitches in bikinis. Even though I was on the set of a music video for the first time in my life, having fun was the last fuckin' thing on my mind. I'd spent the entire night in my room trying to figure out what to do about this shit I'd gotten myself into. After some serious thought, I concluded my best bet would be to just play it cool, bide my time until we got back to NY, and then make my move (whatever it would be).

"Yeah, my man, this is your first video." Scorch flashed a sly grin, adjusting his dick in his wet swimming shorts. "I'm sure your acting skills are just as good as your other skills."

I ice grilled him and put on a fake smile. I raised the bottle of Cristal in my hand, fantasizing about smashing it over that nigga's head. For the rest of the shoot I had to force myself to act like I was in to it, waving bottles in the air and pouring champagne on girls' breasts. I turned off my brain and went through the motions like a soulless zombie, flashing diamond-encrusted watches and glittering necklaces at the camera. I felt angry and sick to my stomach just being in the same vicinity as Scorch. This should've been a dream come true, but it felt more like a nightmare come to life.

Once the scene finally wrapped up, it was around four in the afternoon.

"Alright, fellas, good work," Scorch said, drying himself off with a fluffy towel. "I'm going to stay behind and oversee the rest of the video shoot, but you all are free to go if you like."

"Cool," Tommy Gunn said, taking another swig from his bottle. "I got some bitches waiting for me back home." This was my chance to get the hell out of here.

"Yo, you think I can get a ride with you to the airport, bruh?" I asked.

"Yeah, son. Of course," he replied.

"You bouncing, Wicked?" Scorch said, his arm around a smiling big-tittied chick. "You sure you don't want to stay and chill with us?"

I had to fight the urge to drag his ass to the pool and hold his head under water. "Nah, I gotta get back home to take care of some business."

"Alright, I hear you. I'll see you tomorrow at the studio. Be ready to spit," he paused and squeezed the girl's ass, "on the mic."

I glared at him. "Yeah...aight."

After dapping him up, Tommy and I got dressed and then left the house. When we got outside, I saw a red Maserati parked along the curb. Tommy pulled a set of keys out of the pocket of his sagging jeans and clicked a button. The alarm deactivated with a loud chirp. I'd expected to see a driver, but there wasn't one.

"You're driving?" I looked at him with a raised eyebrow.

"Of course, nigga," he said grinning. "I don't need nobody to chauffer me and shit." The way he was slurring his words and staggering a little, I could tell he was fucked up.

"You want me to drive?" I didn't know shit about Miami, but I was sure an expensive ass car like this had a good navigation system.

Tommy laughed. "Man, if you don't get your ass in the passenger seat and be quiet." He got into the driver side and started the engine.

I opened the passenger side door and got in. I was risking my life with this drunk nigga behind the wheel, but it was a risk that I was willing to take to get away from Scorch. Tommy put the car in gear and pulled off, speeding down the road. He was fast and reckless. My heart was practically in my fuckin' throat as he weaved through the streets, never taking his foot off the gas.

When we finally came to a stop, I decided this would be the perfect opportunity to bring up what was on my mind. "So…Scorch is involved in drug traffickin'?" Tommy seemed a lot more laid back and accessible than Harlem Hood, so I figured he would be open to discussing our powermad boss. I also hoped I could possibly turn him against Scorch.

He glanced at me with a blank expression. "Oh, so he already dropped the other shoe on you?"

"Last night," I said, feeling the anger well up in me as I relived the humiliation I'd been subjected to.

He grunted and didn't say anything.

"You're cool with him involving you in this shit?"

He shrugged his shoulders. "It is what is. It's a small price to pay for living the life-- fucking bad bitches, driving fly cars, and doing whatever the fuck I want, when I want."

I couldn't believe how nonchalant he seemed. "But what if we get caught?"

"We won't. That nigga Scorch is untouchable."

I shook my head. "This shit is crazy, yo."

"Don't worry, mah niggah. As long as everybody on the team does their part and remains loyal, there won't be no problems." When he reached across me and opened the glove compartment to grab a pack of Black & Mild's, I could see a Glock tucked underneath some papers. He closed the compartment and made eye contact with me. "Feel me?"

"Yeah…I hear you," I said, nodding my head. *Loud and clear*.

Once I touched down at JFK in New York four hours later, I caught a cab to Manhattan. My nerves and mind were all over the place. I was mad paranoid. It was clear that I couldn't talk against Scorch to any other member of the Fiyah Spitta Camp. I knew there was only one person I could turn to.

"Yo, Wicked," Ricardo said when I walked into the lobby of Max's building.

"I need to see Max," I said urgently, interrupting him before he could start talking about some random shit. "Is he here?"

"Man," he looked at me from behind the desk, a grim expression on his round face, "you don't know?"

My forehead crinkled. "Know what?"

"Max…he…he was shot last night. He's in the hospital."

CHAPTER 12

"Where to, buddy?" The Pakistani cab driver asked after I slid into the backseat of his taxi and closed the door.

"Mount Sinai Hospital." I leaned back, resting my head against the seat. I was dropping mad money by taking cabs all over the place like I was one of them white bitches on *Sex and the City*, but I didn't give a fuck. At that moment, I didn't care about money. I didn't care about music. I didn't care about anything besides Max. *God, please let him be okay.*

We drove through the city, the nighttime lights of Manhattan flickering through the windows. The radio was on Power 97 and DJ Flipp was talking about Max in a somber voice.

DJ Flipp: "We have a special guest calling in by phone right now. Scorch, welcome to the show."
Scorch: "Thanks for having me, Flipp." His tone was soft and sullen.
DJ Flipp: "I know this must be tough for you. How're you feelin' right now, man?"
Scorch exhaled dramatically.
Scorch: "Yes, this is a very trying time for the entire Fiyah Spitta Family. I'm asking everybody out there to keep Max and his family in your

thoughts and prayers. I still can't believe something like this happened."

Scorch sounded as if he were getting choked up. Flipp remained silent for a minute, allowing him time to "regain" his composure. I felt sick and angry. This was clearly a fucking act, and Flipp was eating it up with a big spoon.

DJ Flipp: "Are you gonna be okay? Where are you right now?"

Scorch: "I...I'm good. I'm just trying to keep it together and be strong for my family, y'know? I was at a video shoot in Miami--of course, I suspended filming as soon as I found out. I'm currently in a car headed to the airport to return to NYC. Once I get back, I intend to offer a sizable reward for anybody who has any info that will lead to the arrest of those *****" (The producer bleeped out his curse word.) *"Sorry about that Flipp; I didn't mean to curse on the air. As you can imagine, I'm kind of beside myself and in a state of shock right now."*

DJ Flipp: "Yeah, yeah, I feel you, man. All of us in the hip-hop community are. How are the other members of your camp taking it?"

Scorch: "We're all hurting, Flipp." (He paused and took a deep breath.) *"Look...I can't talk right now. I just want to say: Max, my man, we love you. And we need you to stay strong and pull through for us. Everybody, please show your love and support for Maximus by logging on to Twitter and--"*

"Aye, can you cut that off?" I snapped at the driver. I couldn't stomach hearing another second of Scorch's phony bullshit.

"Sure, sure, buddy. I turn off." He reached down and hit a button. "No radio now, OK?"

We drove the rest of the way in silence.

Once I arrived at the hospital where Ricardo told me they'd taken Max, I rushed inside and was met by Max's mother in the lobby. I'd called her in the cab and spoke to her briefly on the way to the hospital.

"Hey, Mom." Growing up, Max and I were so close we even called each other's mother "Mom."

Ms. Reeves gave me a tight hug. "How are you, Will?"

"I'm fine...I guess," I replied. "How is he?"

"The bullets punctured a lung and some other vital organs. The doctor operated on him last night, but he said his condition is still serious. It's a fifty-fifty chance he's going to recover." I winced at her words. "This is so horrible." Her eyes were red and puffy with dark circles underneath. She dabbed at them with a crumpled piece of tissue. "I can't believe somebody would do something like this to my baby." She broke down in my arms. I just held her, doing my best to remain strong and fight back my own tears.

Ricardo had told me he heard two guys had ambushed Max while he was on the way to his car at a parking garage a few blocks from his building. They'd supposedly shot him multiple times. It was a miracle he was still here, clinging to life. Once she regained her composure, I broke the silence.

"What did the cops say?"

"Not much. Since Max's jewelry and money were missing, they're treating it as a robbery." She shook her and sighed. "They took what they wanted; it wasn't no need to shoot him like that."

I had a strong hunch this was more than just a robbery, but I didn't want to further upset here with my suspicions. "Can I see him?"

"Of course. Jackie is up there visiting him, too." Jackie was Max's ex-girlfriend and baby mother.

I hastily got on the elevator. My heart beat a mile a minute as it carried me up to the ICU. When the elevator stopped and the doors slid open, I hurried through the sterile, strange-scented white corridors. My stomach was in knots. As soon as I turned the corner and entered his room, I saw Jackie sitting by his bedside.

I took a deep breath and called her named. "Jackie."

She startled at the sound of my voice. Her face relaxed when she realized it was me. "Oh, hey, Wicked." She stood up and came to give me a hug. "It's good to see you again."

"Likewise. I just wish it wasn't under such fucked up circumstances."

"I know. Me and Maxine flew in as soon as Ms. Reeves broke the news to me." Maxine was Max's daughter.

"Maxine's here? Where is she?"

"No, she's at my brother's house. I didn't want her to see him like this." She glanced over her shoulder with an anxious look on her face.

She seemed nervous, but I just chalked it up to stress. "How's Max doing?"

"Still fighting for his life."

I forced myself to look at him. He was hooked up to machines with tubes in his arm and nose.

"Man, this is so messed up." My heart felt heavy as I approached his bed. I shuddered when I saw him up close. He was deathly still. The only movement I saw was his heavily bandaged chest and abdomen slowly rising and falling with the aid of a ventilator.

"Yo, Max," I said softly. I was so tempted to caress his face and run my fingers along his rugged jawline, but I knew Jackie didn't know about us. She was going through enough right now; I didn't want to make her burden even heavier. It tore me up inside that I couldn't touch him. Instead, I just looked at him silently, feeling tears well in my eyes. He was so strong, but now, lying here unconscious, he seemed so frail, so weak. I wanted to nudge him and wake him so badly, and tell him I was sorry for not listening to him about Scorch. I wanted to apologize for everything. A tear rolled down my cheek. I wiped it away with the back of my hand. I felt like shit.

"Scorch had something to do with this," Jackie said out the blue, as if she'd read my mind.

I turned, giving her a peculiar look. "Why do you say that?"

"Max constantly told me that Scorch was grimy. He'd been acting real paranoid for the past few months — insisting Maxine and I move down south to protect us. He didn't tell me much, but he swore it was for our own good, and it was only temporary. I didn't want to move since all of my family is up here. I fought him tooth and nail, but when I saw how adamant he was, I trusted him and took his word for it."

I frowned, realizing if I'd just trusted Max too about Scorch, none of this would probably be happening.

"A few days before the shooting, he told me he was worried for his life."

"Did he tell you why?"

"He said he was working with some people who wanted to take Scorch down."

"Did he say who?"

She looked like she wanted to say more, but wasn't certain if she should.

"Who is it? You can tell me."

"The only one he mentioned by name was Harlem Hood."

"Are you serious?" I stared at her incredulously. I would've sworn if anyone was loyal to Scorch, it would be Hood, considering he was the first artist signed to the label. "Did he say what they were plannin' to do?"

She shook her no. "He refused to go into details about it." Of course.

"I feel the same way you do. In my gut, I have a feelin' that this is Scorch's doing." It was no coincidence that this had happened right before Max was supposed to meet me. I was suddenly hit with a frightening thought. "If he is really behind this, he may try to send someone to finish the job."

"He's safe. The hospital already has him in a special wing with added security because he's a celebrity."

"Good." I gave Max a lingering look. "Don't let anyone else from Scorcher see him, okay?"

"Alright."

I placed a hand on her shoulder. "Don't worry. I'm goin' to take care of this."

*****

Jackie and Ms. Reeves were going to take turns staying at the hospital waiting for an update from Max's doctor. I asked them if they wanted me to stay, but both insisted I go home and get some rest. I reluctantly left the hospital, feeling like I had the weight of the world on my shoulders. Even though I didn't want to leave Max's side, I knew they right. I wouldn't do any good by staying there and stressing myself out worrying. Max's fate was in God's hands now.

However, Scorch's fate was about to be in mine. I was goin' to make him pay for what he'd done. Even though I didn't care for Harlem Hood, I realized he could potentially be an ally. I had to get in touch with him. But how? I hadn't seen him since the night of my signing party. I had to figure out a way to get his number without asking Scorch or Tommy. I didn't want to raise any red flags by contactin' other members of the camp.

As I walked towards the nearest train station, snow flurries began to fall. It was brick outside. I crossed a brightly lit avenue and turned onto a dark street. Save for a stray cat skulking about and a few people passing by, the block was relatively empty.

"Yo, Wicked."

I startled at the voice that had called my name from the darkness. I turned to see two dudes dressed in all black emerge from the shadows. As their silhouettes became visible under the dim street lights, I instantly recognized them. It was the two niggas I'd seen before; once at Max's place several weeks ago, and again at the club. *What the fuck are they doing here???*

I tensed up, balled my fists, and prepared myself for whatever was about to go down.

"Relax, man. We're not here to cause problems," the tall dreadhead said. "My name is Driggs." He thumbed over his shoulder at the dude with the bald head and the bushy beard standing behind him. "This is Kane."

"Yeah, I've seen you around before." I eyed them warily. "What do you want?"

"We just wanna talk to you real quick."

"About what?" I still wasn't feelin' this dude's vibe.

"I'd rather not discuss it out here. There's a diner nearby. Can we go there to talk?"

"Nah, I don't think so, bruh." I looked at him like he was stupid. "I don't know ya'll; so why should I go anywhere with you?"

"Because we're friends of Max."

"Did Scorch send you?"

"No."

"So if you don't work for Scorch, then who do you work for?"

"Someone who wants to take him down probably as much as you do right about now." He just stood there gazing at me intently, as if waiting for me to change my mind. I didn't say shit. I wasn't takin' the bait. I had no idea who these niggas were or what their agenda was. Them just showing up here out the blue was too convenient. Hell, for all I knew, they could've been the niggas who shot Max. When Driggs realized I wasn't going to reply, he scrubbed a hand across his scruffy face. "Aight, I guess you don't wanna talk right now. It's understandable. After what happened to your boy, I don't blame you. Take my number and holla at me later, alright?"

I shook my head, keeping my eyes locked on them. "Nah...I'm good."

"Okay. I'm sure you'll change your mind." He twisted his lips into a subtle smirk. "Be safe out here, boss."

Without another word, they turned and walked up the block. I watched them disappear around the corner before unclenching my fists and allowing my body to relax a little. I realized I could've easily been laid out on the sidewalk bleeding to death if those dudes had been gunnin' for me. I was usually aware of my surroundings at all times, but with everything that had happened in the last 24 hours, I was slippin'. They'd obviously followed me all the way from the hospital without me noticing. Judging by those two shifty muthafuckas who claimed to be Max's friends, it was clear he was mixed up in some seriously shady shit. I had a bad feeling the whole drug trafficking thing he'd hidden from me may have just been the tip of the iceberg.

CHAPTER 13

I arrived at the label offices the following afternoon with an agenda.

"You're here early," Scorch's assistant, Darlene, said when she saw me approaching her station. "The meeting doesn't start for another hour."

She'd called me in for a meeting at Scorch's request.

"Yeah, I know." I gave her a warm smile. "How you feelin' today?"

She smiled back. "All things considered, I'm okay. I'm still shaken up about Max."

"Same here. Is Scorch in his office?"

"No, he's not here yet."

"Do you know if Harlem Hood is goin' to be at the meeting?"

She shook her head. "Nope. You're the only artist Shameek asked me to call in."

I wondered what was up with that. Fuck. I'd hope to see Hood here and possibly get him alone somewhere to talk. "Aye, I need to ask you a favor."

Her eyebrows quirked upward. "What?"

"Can you give me Hood's number?"

"I don't know, Wicked." She nervously chewed her bottom lip. "I can get in trouble for that."

"Come on, ma. It's important. Don't worry, this is just between me and you. I won't tell him how I got it." I stared into her eyes and gave her a smooth smile. "Please?"

After a little more flirting and begging, I finally got her to come up off of Hood's digits. I went outside and walked a couple blocks down from the building to make the phone call.

It rang until Hood's voicemail picked up.

Shit. It was too risky to leave a message. I would try again later. Just as I was about to pocket my phone, it started ringing. I looked at the caller ID and saw the call was coming from a blocked number. For a second, I wondered if I should I answer it.

"Hello?"

"Who's this?" I instantly recognized Hood's distinctive, gravelly voice.

"Wicked."

"What do you want?"

"I need to talk to you. It's about Max."

"Yeah, I already know he's in the hospital."

"No, not that. I wanna talk about who put him there."

A few seconds of silence passed before he spoke again.

"How did you get my number?"

"Max." I had no choice but to wing it and hope for the best. "He gave it to me a few days ago; he told me if anything happened to him, I should call."

Another long stretch of silence passed. "Where are you?"

I hesitated to reply, not sure if I should tell him the truth.

"Nevermind. Look, when's the soonest you can be at the corner of 10th and 48th St?"

"Uh, I'm not in the city right now," I lied. I knew if I told him I was about to attend a meeting with Scorch, he might become suspicious and change his mind about talking to me. I looked at my watch and guestimated the amount of time I would need. "I can be there by noon."

"Come alone." He abruptly ended the call.

When I walked into the conference room where the meeting was being held, the heads of each department and some office support staff were already seated at a large circular table. The mood in the room was somber. Everyone had long faces. Scorch entered the room not too long after me and took his seat at the head of the table. He promptly called the meeting to order. He spent a little time talking about Max before moving on to other things, such as record sales and promotional projects. He was all business. His legit mogul persona was nothing like the vindictive version of him I'd encountered the other night. I doubted any of these people outside of his inner circle the Fiyah Spitta Crew had any clue what was going on behind the scenes. Whenever he made eye contact with me, I looked away, trying not to show my hatred. As he was wrapping up the meeting, I still couldn't help wonder why I was the only artist here.

"So in conclusion, I know this is a tough day for all of us, but we have to stay focused and continue doing what we do best: Being the hottest record label on the planet. Max would want it that way." He stood up and leaned forward, resting his knuckles on the table. "Alright everyone, back to work."

Everyone got up and began filing out the room.

"Wicked, I want to talk to you for a minute," Scorch said. Once the room cleared out, he closed and locked the door. He then came over and sat down on the table top next to me. "Look, the reason why I called you to this staff meeting is because I wanted to apologize for how I came at you last night. I didn't mean to disrespect you like that. I know it's no excuse, but I was pretty fucked up. I don't want you to think poorly of me because of my behavior. I don't want what happened to damage our partnership."

"It's all good. We were twisted; we both probably said and did some shit we didn't mean. Don't even sweat it."

"I'm glad you understand." He smiled and shook my hand. "The second thing I wanted to talk to you about is Max. I went by the hospital to visit him before I came here, but his girl turned me away."

"Word?" I asked, acting surprised. "Why?"

"Apparently, she's under the crazy impression that I had something to do with what happened to him."

"Are you?"

He looked offended. "Of course not."

"Well, you did threaten me with bodily harm if I tried to leave the label. Not to mention, you had that big nigga Byron pull a gun on me. After all that, setting somebody up sounds like something you might be capable of."

"I told you that was just the liquor talking. And that was after you hit me first. I freely admit, I shot off my mouth and Byron overacted. I'd never harm anybody on my team though. You all are my family."

I looked down at the table and didn't respond.

"I know this must be rough for you." He'd revealed the other night that he already knew about me and Max's relationship, but I never got the opportunity to ask him how.

"How did you find out about us anyway?"

"When you called me out the blue, I knew you had to have gotten my number from somebody on my team. After we met, I had someone do a little digging on you. In the process, they discovered a link between you and Max. It was nothing to pay people around Max for more information. The guy who works security at his building, I believe his name is Ricardo, was quite helpful in that regard. He provided some rather valuable info on the comings and goings at Max's apartment."

Holy shit! Ricardo was an informant for Scorch???

"So not only were you spying on him, but you paid someone to take him out, too?"

He stood up and narrowed his eyes.

"You don't have to answer. I don't really care one way or the other."

Scorch gave me a puzzled look. I could tell he was shocked by my admission.

I rose from my chair, holding his gaze. "Keeping it one hundred--I was just using him to get to you anyway. That nigga never cared about my career. He even admitted to me that he tried to talk you out of signing me."

"Yes, he did try to discourage me from giving you a shot."

We were standing face to face, only inches apart. "Fuck that snake nigga, yo." I grabbed his dick through his slacks. It was on brick. "I like cats with power."

"Oh yeah?" He licked his lips, staring hard in my eyes.

"Word." I massaged his dick.

"I knew you would come around."

"Because you know I'm an ambitious nigga, just like you, right? The only thing I care about is getting to the top. By any means necessary. And I'm smart enough to know the quickest way to do me…is by doing you." I placed a hand on his chest, gripping his necktie. I gently pulled him into me, pressing my lips to his. I moaned softly as he aggressively kissed me back. I broke the kiss and gave him a seductive look. He stared back at me lustfully. I could tell he would've fucked me right there on the conference table if I let him. "But we shouldn't mix business with pleasure, boss man. They'll be plenty of time for pleasure when we have more privacy."

"True. We'll finish this later."

"No doubt." I bit my bottom lip, continuing to flirt with him. I had something he wanted, and I intended to use it to my advantage. Keep your friends close, and your enemies even closer. Gain his confidence. Make him drop his guard a little.

Like we say in the streets; I was going to rock him to sleep. And when the time was right, I was goin' to fuck his ass all the way up.

After leaving the office, I hopped on the nearest train headed downtown. It was already a quarter to noon. When I got to 10th avenue and W 48th St it was a few minutes after twelve. I stood on the corner in front of a Dunkin Donuts freezing, trying to be inconspicuous while I looked about. What was I looking for? I had no fuckin' idea.

Seconds later, a black Mercedes pulled up to the curb and came to a slow stop. Two dudes were in the car. The passenger side window rolled down. A man with shades stared me up and down before finally speaking.

"Get in."

"Who are you?"

"Hood sent us. If you want to talk to him, get in."

I eyed them with suspicion. "Where he is?"

"Are you coming, or not?" His tone was impatient.

I looked around again, and then cautiously reached for the door handle. I got in back and closed the door. When I heard the locks suddenly click, I wondered if I'd made a huge mistake.

CHAPTER 14

"The two big men led me through the hallway of an expensive hotel not far away. One walked in front of me, and the other brought up the rear. Neither of them had uttered a word the entire way here. Based on the way they were dressed, I assumed they were Hood's security guards. Or, at least I prayed that's who they were.

"You have any weapons on you?" The one in front turned and asked me out the blue.

"Uh, nah."

He grunted and kept walking.

Man, what the hell have I gotten myself into?

Once we got to a certain room number, the dude with the shades knocked on the door three times in a way that seemed like a special code. A few seconds later, the door opened. Hood stood there with a scowl on his face. He moved to the side to allow us entry, and then closed and locked the door behind us.

"Did Scorch send you?"

"What?" I laughed a little.

The look on his face told me he wasn't joking.

"No, of course not."

He glanced at the two dudes. "Check him."

Before I even knew what was happening, they started patting me up and down my body with their big paws. I scrunched my face.

"He's good," one of them said to Hood.

"What the fuck, yo?" I glared at him.

"Relax, bruh. I just had to make sure you weren't a hired a gun," Hood said. "After what Scorch did to Max, I have to be careful."

"So, you believe he was behind the shooting, too?"

"I know he was. It's his MO. He must've somehow discovered that me and Max were plotting on him, and struck back at us. I've been laying low ever since it happened. That's why I wasn't at Malicious' video shoot."

"Damn." I rubbed the back of my neck and remained quiet, letting everything sink in. "The way you told Tommy not to discuss business in public when he was running off at the mouth, I thought for sure you were riding hard with Scorch."

"I only said that to throw Tommy off. Him and Malicious have their lips attached to Scorch's ass cheeks. They can't be trusted."

"And you can?" I raised a skeptical eyebrow. "You've been with him longer than any of us."

"True. I've been with that nigga since the beginning. I sold millions of records for his company. I helped put his label on the map. I even helped establish his drug traffickin' side hustle. I always had that nigga's back, never once going against him. And what the fuck do I have to show for it? Nothing!" He grimaced. "That nigga took advantage of me, locking me in a shitty long-term deal. He's been making mad money off me all these years, but my royalty rate still ain't changed. He refuses to release me from my contract. Homeboy's gone mad with power; paying people to follow whoever he suspects is against him and probably even bugging shit. It's like modern-day slavery."

He was being dramatic comparing his life to slavery, but whatever; I didn't call him on it. "So, what's your plan to take him down?"

"Simple." He stared me in the eye, a sinister grin parting his pink lips. "Kill him."

My blood ran cold. "Are you serious? You're going to kill Scorch?"

He nodded his head.

"Max was down with that?" There was no way I would believe Max would be desperate or stupid enough to go along with a murder plot.

"Not exactly. Originally, the plan was to secretly gather together enough of us who were fed up with Scorch's shit and threaten to walk; hopefully forcing him to release us from our contracts without retaliation. But after what happened to Max, things have changed. Shit just got real. The only thing that's going to stop him is a bullet to the head. I don't know for sure if he realizes I was plotting with Max or not, but I ain't taking no chances—I'm going to get him before he gets me. If you're smart, you'd join me."

Well, he definitely *sounded* like he hated Scorch as much as I did. But I still didn't know if I could fully trust him. "Did you send Driggs and Kane to recruit me?"

"Who?" He gave me a weird look.

"These two niggas approached me last night after I left the hospital visiting Max. They said they were working with Max to take Scorch down, too."

He shook his head. "I don't know who they are, but I'm not surprised others are gunning for him. Ole boy has made a lot of enemies over the years."

"Maybe there's another way to handle this other than killing him?"

"Like what—go to the police?" Hood scoffed, glancing at his bodyguards. They both just stood there stonefaced. "Snitchin' to the cops wouldn't be a good look for our careers, bruh."

I couldn't believe we were dealing with life and death, and this nigga was only worried about his street cred. I thought for a minute, trying to come up with something he might go for. "What if we went on the radio and put him on blast?" He gave me a look that seemed to suggest he thought I was crazy or stupid.

He sucked his teeth. "Man, fuck outta here."

"Nah, hear me out," I tried to explain. "If we do that, he wouldn't dare touch us."

"And why not?"

"Because if something happened to either one of us after we publicly accuse him, he knows all eyes would instantly be on him. He wouldn't want to risk the police attention."

He fanned his hand at me dismissively. "Like them cops would give a rat's ass if you or I came up missing. It'd just be one less rap nigga for them to worry about. They'd file the case away before we even made it to the morgue. Hell, they still ain't found out who shot Biggie and Pac yet. And Scorch would just put out an album of our unreleased music so he can continue making money off of us and keep it moving. Just like Puffy and Suge did with Pac and Big."

I mulled his words. He did have a point. "Aight...so maybe we can tip off the police anonymously about this drug traffickin' shit he's involved in?"

"No fuckin' police!" He yelled. "We're going to cap that nigga. Case closed."

I sucked in a deep breath and massaged my throbbing temples. This shit was crazy. I felt like I was in between a rock and a hard place.

"Are you in or out?"

"Nah, I'm not down with this man. You can do what you want. Count me out." I would figure out my own way to take Scorch down without stooping to his level. I had too much respect for life. Even one as grimy as Scorch's. For me, murder was a last resort.

"When I first met you at the club, I was suspicious of you. Max swore you had no allegiance to Scorch even though you'd just signed a deal with him. Although he said you could be trusted, he didn't want to bring you in our plans. Now I see why." He smirked. "Cause you straight pussy, son."

"What the fuck did you say?" I walked up to him and got in his face.

"You heard me." He shoved my chest. "I don't know why Max thought we could trust your PUNK ASS!" He took a wild swing at me. I sidestepped it and dropped him with a punch to the jaw. I jumped on top of him and started swingin'.

"Aye! Aye!" The guard with the shade's said as he pulled me off of Hood. "That's enough."

Like any real punk who just got his ass beat, Hood couldn't accept a L in stride. "Nah, yo. This is ain't over. I'm gonna smoke this nigga!" He staggered to his feet, lifted his shirt and reached for a gun. Before he could pull it from his waistband, the other dude grabbed him from behind. "Man, get the fuck off!" His face turned bright red and spittle flew from his mouth as he snarled liked a rabid dog. "Nigga, you work for me!" He trashed about, struggling to break free.

"Man, ya'll already up here making mad noise and shit. If you fire a gun in this building, you know someone's gonna call the cops. They'll be swarming the lobby before we even get downstairs," the guy said, still restraining Hood.

His words seemed to register with him, and he reluctantly began to settle down.

"You cool?" Shades asked him, still holding me in a bearhug.

"Yeah...I'm straight," Hood replied, pulling his arm free of his guard's grasp. "You can let him go."

Shades finally loosened his grip on me.

"Look, we're both obviously stressed the fuck out right now, so I'm going to act like that fight didn't just happen," Hood said, his voice calm again. "Scorch is who we should be focusing our animosity towards."

I grimaced, not saying a word.

"We don't have to like each other to work together." He slowly extended his hand to me. "So I'm asking you again…are you in or out?"

"I'll think about it," I replied, leaving him hanging.

"What you mean--'You'll think about it'?" He withdrew his hand and twisted his lips. "Max told me you all were tight. You just gonna let that nigga Scorch pop your manz like that and get away with it? That's some bitch shit right there, yo."

"Trust me. He's not gettin' away with shit on my watch."

"So what the fuck are you gonna do then?"

"I'm goin' to handle shit my own way." I pushed past him and started for the door.

"Yo, where the fuck you think you going?"

"Don't worry 'bout that, son."

Shades rushed over and stood in front of the door, blocking my path. I stared up at him. Dude had to be about 6'5.

"You better not mention none of this shit to Scorch," Hood said.

I turned my head in his direction, locking eyes with him. "Nigga, I'm not stupid."

"Could've fooled me," he sniffed.

"Can I go now?" I asked drily.

He gave me a lingering look, and then motioned his head at Shades, causing him to move aside. Just as I was about to reach for the door handle, Hood started poppin' shit again. "You gonna regret not joining up with me when you had the chance."

I walked out the door without saying another word. I wasn't goin' to let Hood manipulate me by getting under my skin. I got on the elevator and pushed the button to the lobby. As it began to go down, I leaned with my back against the wall and shut my eyes. I honestly had no idea how I could take someone as powerful as Scorch down, but he definitely had to be stopped. However, the thought of murdering him didn't sit well with me. The prospect of getting caught, serving a life sentence, and not being around to help raise my son scared the shit out of me.

When I got back to my crib, mom dukes was sitting in the living room watching TV.

"Hey, ma," I said, taking note of the serious expression on her face. "What's wrong?"

She looked up at me from her recliner. "Two men came here a little while ago looking for you."

"For me? Did they say who they were?"

"Nope. They just said they needed to talk to you. One of them had dreadlocks."

My heart plummeted to my stomach. Driggs.

"He asked me to give you this." She pulled a folded piece of paper from her housecoat and handed it to me.

I unfolded the handwritten note and read it silently:

We're meeting up later to plan. If you decide you're down, text me, and I'll hit you back with the time and place.

At the bottom was a phone number and Driggs' signature underneath it. I folded it back up and shoved it in my pocket.

"What's that all about?" Knowing how nosey my mother is, I knew she'd probably already read the note.

"Nothin'. Just some guys from the label lookin' to get up with me."

She didn't seem convinced. "Do they have any updates on the people who shot Max?"

"Nah," I said with a grim expression.

She shook her head ruefully. "I'm sure somebody knows who did it, but they scared to say something."

"Probably." I continued to my room. I was in no mood to talk. Especially when I knew who was behind the shooting. The last thing I wanted to do was involve my mother in any of this madness. Unfortunately, it looked like it was already too late for that.

If Driggs and Kane knew where I rested, they probably knew where my baby mother and son stayed, too. That thought caused a shiver to shoot down my spine. I quickly pulled out my phone and called Tanieka to check on her and Will. I was relieved when she told me nothing out of the ordinary had happened, and no one had approached her recently. They were safe...but for how long? I had to find out who these dudes were and what they wanted before they showed up again. I pulled out the note Driggs had left and punched his digits in my phone. I then sent him a text.

Me: I'll meet u
Several minutes passed before he responded.
Driggs: Good. I'll hit you back in a minute wit time and place
Me: Aight

Later that night, after changing into a hoodie, I dug in my bottom dresser drawer. Buried underneath a bunch of clothes was something I never hoped to use. It was a Smith and Wesson I'd copped from Ronnell a few years back. I wasn't a fan of guns, but desperate times called for desperate measures. I didn't know what I was walkin' into by agreeing to meet up with these cats. I made sure the gun was loaded, and then carefully tucked it in my jeans, covering the handle with my hoodie. I put on my coat and left the house for the train station.

By the time I came up from the subway at my destination, a fast and steady snow had started to fall. I looked from the left to the right. Aside from people scampering about more hurriedly than usual, there didn't appear to be anything out of the ordinary. No one appeared to be trailing me, at least not on foot anyway. That realization did nothing to put me at ease as I looked at all of the occupied cars on the street. Any one of them could contain someone whom Scorch or whoever Driggs was working for paid to follow me.

"Shit," I grumbled. The spot Driggs had texted to meet was supposed to be an inconspicuous little diner where no one would recognize us. It was six blocks away in an area I wasn't too familiar with. I pulled the hoodie over my head and started walking in that direction.

I arrived at the spot ten minutes later. The snow was coming down like a blizzard now. I stood under the awning of a closed storefront a few feet away and surveyed my surroundings. I spotted the small diner at the end of the block. I pulled out my phone and texted him. He instantly replied back, lettin' me know he and Kane were already there. I threw caution to the wind and went inside. Before the hostess at the door could greet me, I saw them posted off in a corner booth.

"I'm here to meet somebody."

Driggs waved me over. I walked back to them and sat down.

"Glad you could join us, Wicked. I knew you would change your mind about talking to us," Driggs said, taking a sip of coffee from his cup. "Can I get you something?"

"Nah, I'm not here for all that. All I wanna know is who do you work for?"

"Wow, straight to the point, aren't you?" He smiled.

"I worked for Scorch until I was sent upstate because of his snake ass," Kane interjected, stroking his beard.

I looked to him with a puzzled expression, prompting him to elaborate.

"I used to be a part of his security team. One night while we were leaving the club, a cop pulled us over. Police searched the SUV and found drugs."

"Yeah, I remember hearing about that incident a few years back. It was in all the papers and shit." I didn't remember all the details, but I did know that Scorch wasn't charged with anything.

"That motherfucker had me take the fall. He promised me if I took the rap for him, he'd get me a good lawyer to get me off. And if worse came to worse and I got convicted, he would financially compensate me for my loyalty and lost time once I got out. Like a chump, I believed him. It was all bullshit. After I copped to the charges, that nigga hung me out to dry and then dropped me like an afterthought." His jaw clenched. "I spent years in that small ass cell dreaming about getting back at that nigga once I got out. I recruited my boy Driggs here to help. Me and him go way back."

Aside from the fact that Driggs seemed to be calling the shots and not the other way around, something didn't add up about his story

"If you've been plottin' on Scorch for a minute now, why haven't you taken him out already?"

"We were biding our time, waiting for the right opportunity. But now that he knows peeps are after him, he's going to be a lot more careful to mask his movements. Getting close to him now will be more difficult."

I knew I could probably get closer to Scorch than anyone, but I wasn't going to tell them that. For now, I would keep those cards close to my vest. I'd done some bad things in my life, but committing murder wasn't one of them. I hoped to never cross that line.

Driggs took another slurp of coffee and set his cup down on the table. "So, what do ya say? You want to help us take him out?"

"The only thing I have to say is, don't bring your asses around my crib anymore."

"Or what?" Driggs said, narrowing his eyes at me.

I leaned back in my seat and lifted up my hoodie a little, exposing the handle of my gun. "Don't try me, bruh."

He smirked. "So, it's like that, huh?"

"Yep." I stood up and calmly walked out the diner. I pulled the hoodie back over my head as I exited back into the cold night. I kept lookin' back over my shoulder, expecting to see them following me at any moment. Once I got outside, I lingered in front just waiting on their asses to step foot out the diner and try me. After a few minutes passed and they didn't, I assumed I had gotten my point across. Casting a final glance at the door, I turned and began walking away. Before I got to the end of the block, three black cars pulled up out of nowhere.

My heart thundered in my chest.

I started to reach for my gun.

Red and blue lights flashed in the windows.

I heard a "woop, woop" sound. I knew I was fucked.

These weren't hitmen cars. They were unmarked police cruisers.

The doors swung open and a bunch of guys jumped out with guns drawn.

"Put your hands in the air!" One of the men with a bushy mustache barked, pointing his gun at me.

"Fuck!" I shouted under my breath. I reluctantly raised my hands. Three plain clothes cops swarmed me, tackling me to the wet pavement and piling on top of me. The side of my face was mushed against the cold concrete curb. I felt a knee in my back and hands patting me down. My arms were then yanked behind me, and my wrists handcuffed. They rolled me over and patted my front pockets. After unzipping my coat, one of them snatched up the front of my hoodie and grabbed the gun from my waist. Two officers gripped me by the arms and pulled me to my feet. The one with the bushy mustache approached me and flashed his badge in my face.

"You're under arrest."

Before I could protest, he started reading me my Miranda rights.

CHAPTER 15

I looked around at the dingy walls of the small room and impatiently rapped my fingers on the table. It had been an hour, or maybe even longer, since they brought me in this room and left me alone. I'd lost track of time and wasn't sure how long I'd been here. The only thing I knew for certain was that I'd been setup. But by whom? That was the question. Was it Hood? Scorch? Or both? I was so fucking confused and disoriented, I didn't know what to think or believe anymore. Ever since I went behind Max's back to sign with Scorch, my life had been turned upside down. I halfway expected Max to walk into the room with a big smile on his face and tell me this was all some elaborate practical joke to teach me a lesson. I would've given anything for that to happen. Unfortunately, two men in black suits and white shirts with ties walked in the room instead.

"Good evening, Mr. Marshall," the white dude said. "I'm Agent Myers, with the FBI." He motioned to the black guy. "This is Detective Lamar."

"I'm with the NYPD Crime Reduction Unit," Lamar said. They both pulled up a chair and sat across from me. "Do you know why you're here tonight, Mr. Marshall?"

I shook my head. "Nope. But I guess you're gonna tell me, right?"

"You're here because of your involvement with Scorcher Records. More specifically, because of your association with its owner, Shameek 'Scorch' Sampson. Various law enforcement agencies have been investigating and building a case against Scorch for years for numerous offenses ranging from drug distribution to murder. As you are undoubtedly aware, his label is just an arm and an extension of a vast criminal empire."

"Nah, I didn't know that," I lied. I wasn't copping to shit. I was a second away from invoking my right not to speak without a lawyer present, when Myers spoke.

"Well, your friend Maximus knew, which is why he was helping us bring Scorch down. We'd been working with him for the past few months to infiltrate Scorcher Records." Max was working with the Feds and didn't want me to know? That explained his erratic and secretive behavior! He was actually trying to keep me out of this insanity.

"Yeah, and look where that got him." I was treading on shaky ground by being so combative, but I wasn't about to let these dudes intimidate me. They'd probably pulled the same stunt with Max to get him to work with them. Just thinking about it made the anger rise up in me. "Working with you guys got him shot."

Lamar gave me a sympathetic look, his face softening. "The situation with Max is unfortunate, and we're diligently working to track down the guys who did it."

"Man, you're actin' like what happened to him is just some random robbery. Scorch set that shit up--it was a hit!"

"I can understand why you feel that way. However, there's currently nothing linking him to the shooting. But if you feel so strongly that Scorch is behind it, perhaps you'd be interested in helping us take him down."

I stared at him skeptically. "How?"

"With Max in the hospital, we need someone else close to Scorch, someone in his inner circle. There's already a solid case against him, but we need something to make it airtight so the charges will stick," Myers chimed in.

"Something like what?" I asked, raising an eyebrow.

"We want him on tape admitting his involvement in illegal drug activities."

"Let me get this straight. Are you askin' me to wear a wire???"

Myers gave me a subtle grin. "Bingo."

"Hell nah," I replied, scrunching my face. "Why don't you get Harlem Hood or another person in the Fiyah Spittas to do it?"

"Because...they're all targets of our investigation as well."

I leaned back in my chair and folded my arms over my chest. "And why the fuck should I help you?"

"In exchange for your full cooperation, we'll speak to the DA on your behalf, and see what we can do to mitigate any potential charges. But if you choose not to cooperate, just know that once Scorch goes down, you'll go down with him."

"For what?"

"Conspiracy to commit murder," Lamar said.

"Who did I conspire to murder?"

"Don't play dumb with us, Will," Myers interjected, bringing his fist down on the table top.

"You don't have anything on me," I said with defiance in my voice.

"Kane and 'Driggs' work for us," he replied smugly. *An informant and an undercover. It fuckin' figures.* "You went to meet with them under the assumption they were plotting a murder."

"So?" I shrugged. "I just went to hear what they had to say to stop them from harassing me. I never agreed to anything."

Myers exhaled through his nose, his face beginning to flush. I could tell by his irritated expression and the way his lips twisted, he knew I was right. Even though they'd tried to entrap me, I hadn't said or done anything incriminating.

Lamar placed his hands on the table and leaned in, making eye contact with me. "If a murder conspiracy charge doesn't stick, the DA can come up with something else to charge you with. In case you've forgotten, we did find a gun on your person at the time of your arrest. Even if we don't get you on a serious charge, I'm sure you're aware sentences for illegal firearm possession here in the state of New York can also be rather lengthy? Just let that sink in for a minute."

I lowered my head and frowned. He had me. Even with the cash advance I'd gotten from signing my record deal, there was no way I would be able to afford the high-priced attorneys needed to fight state and possibly federal charges. I let out a frustrated sigh. I was SOL...damned if I did, and damned if I didn't.

CHAPTER 16

When I walked out of jail, I just stood there for a moment letting the sun caress my skin. After being locked up for several days, it felt good to see it in the sky and feel its warmth again. As I stretched, I noticed a black Escalade with tinted windows parked a few feet away. The door opened. Will lept out and sprinted up to me, jumping into my arms.

"Sup, Michelangelo?" I said, squeezing him tightly.

He pulled back. "Daddy, I'm Leonardo today."

"My bad, yo," I said, laughing.

He frowned. "I thought I wasn't ever gonna see you again."

My brow furrowed. "Why not?"

"Mommy said you were probably goin' to prison for a long time."

"She did, huh?" I glanced up to see Tanieka getting out the truck and making her way over to us. From her irritated expression, I could already see she had an attitude. I hated involving her in this, but I needed someone to make the call to Scorch for me while I was behind bars.

"I can't believe this, Wicked." She shook her head. "You just signed a big record deal and yet you still out here getting caught up in dumb shit. What the hell were you thinking?"

"Can we do this later?" I asked, still holding Will. "I don't want to talk about this right now."

She rolled her eyes and started walking back to the truck. I followed behind her. They slid into the backseat, and I got in after them. Just as expected, Scorch was sitting inside.

"Wassup, bossman?" I said, reaching across Tanieka and Will to dap him up. "I owe you big time for bailing me out."

"Don't mention it." He smiled. "I'm sure you'll repay me later."

"Yeah…no doubt." I faced forward, suddenly feelin' anxious about what I'd agreed to do.

We drove to Tanieka's mother's house in silence. When we pulled up to the curb, I got out to let her and Will out.

"Oh, Tanieka," Scorch called out. "I'll have someone from my office contact you regarding that position in our legal department."

"Thank you, Scorch," she said, cheesing mad hard.

"No problem. And anything little Will needs, don't hesitate to ask his Uncle Scorch."

I felt a spike of anger. I didn't like the idea of him being this close to my family.

"Okay, I will." Tanieka was cheesing even harder. I gave her an incredulous look. She pursed her lips and shrugged her shoulders. *Always looking for a fuckin' come up.* "I'm just trying to look out for our son."

"We'll talk later." I lowered myself so I was eyelevel with my son. "Be good for Mommy, alright. Always remember that Daddy loves you and will always be here for you, okay?"

He seemed a little confused by how sentimental I was actin', but nodded his understanding anyway. I pulled him into a hug and gave him a kiss on the forehead. I smiled grimly and waved goodbye to him as they walked up the driveway. I watched them disappear into the house before getting back in the truck.

"So, you good?" Scorch asked. "Did they treat you alright in there?"

"Yeah, it wasn't too bad. This is all that nigga Harlem Hood's fault."

He raised an eyebrow. "What do you mean?"

"He's workin' with some dudes to set you up, yo. One of them said he used to work for you; some cat who goes by the name of 'Driggs'."

Scorch had a stoic, unreadable expression on his face.

"He tried to get me to join up with them, but I turned him down. Before I could tell you, the cops busted me. I know he tipped them off to get back at me."

"I was aware Max was scheming against me with someone else in my camp, but I would've never suspected Hood. He and I founded this label together. I was always the brains, since I had the industry experience and the business savvy to make shit happen. He was just a dude on the block who I put on. We were always tight...almost like brothers."

"Word?" Their friendship sounded a little like mine and Max's.

"Yeah." He seemed genuinely hurt by Hood's betrayal, but quickly snapped out of it. "These are some serious claims you're making, Wicked."

"I know. Don't take my word for it, though. Ask him yourself. You can't trust these snake niggas out here, bruh. Especially with all the money you pullin' in and shit."

"True." He gave me a contemplative look, as if he was trying to read my mind.

"You can trust me." I rested a hand on his inner thigh and slowly slid it to his crotch. "Like you told me, 'I got you.'"

He groaned softly as I pushed my hand into his pants and started stroking his dick. It instantly got hard. He slid his pelvis forward and leaned his head back against the seat. I continued to jerk him. When I felt him start to precum, I removed my hand from his underwear and licked the precum from my fingers.

A smile spread across his face. "Byron, take us home."

*****

I looked around in awe as Scorch led me through his sprawling upstate mansion. He eventually brought me into what I assumed was the living room, or at least one of them anyway. There was a huge entertainment center and a giant flat screen on the wall, a real fireplace, and even a bar in the corner which appeared to be better stocked than a bar at some clubs. I knew the rich lived well, but damn! While I was busy trippin' over this extravagant setup, Scorch came up behind me and placed a hand on the small of my back. When I turned to face him, he pulled me into his hard body. He lowered his head and started kissing me on the neck. I palmed his dick. It was already growing hard again. He lifted his head and stared into my eyes as he began to unbutton my shirt. He was a second away from kissing me on the lips, when I gently pushed him away.

"What's the rush, yo? We got all the time in the world." I held his gaze as I walked over to the long, white leather sofa and sat down.

"Carpe diem, my man. You never know how long you've got left on this planet. Seize the moment." Scorch chuckled.

"No doubt. I feel you."

"Would you like something to drink?" He made his way to the bar.

"Yeah."

"What do you want? I got everything you can think of."

"I bet you do." I flashed a flirty smile. "Surprise me."

He smiled back, nodding his head. After pouring two drinks, he walked over to me and handed me a glass of brown liquor. I took a sip of it and grimaced, feeling it burn my throat on the way down.

"Cognac." Scorch took a sip from his glass, looking amused. "The good shit. I believe this particular brand runs several thousand a bottle."

"I believe that. It's strong as fuck."

He laughed and sat close to me on the couch. We spent the next thirty minutes drinking and discussing my legal predicament. Scorch assured me that I would beat the gun charge.

"You really think I'll get off?"

"Of course," he said confidently. "I'll set you up with some excellent lawyers."

"Thanks." I had been subtly trying to get him to talk about his drug trafficking operation, but he kept changing the subject. This seemed like the perfect opportunity. "Do you think they could get you off if you ever got caught?"

He gave me a weird look. "Caught for what?"

"You know, the whole drug trafficking thing."

He was about to say something when the doorbell rang. "Oh, I invited someone to join us. Byron," he called out, "can you get that?"

Byron promptly left the room.

A few minutes later, he returned, followed by Hood.

Shit. I wasn't actually expecting him to confront Hood this soon. Scorch moved fast. I didn't even see or hear him give Byron the order to bring him in while we were coming here. *Fuck! This isn't good.* Byron came over and leaned into Scorch. I heard him say in a low voice that Hood was clean.

Scorch set his drink on the table and stood to clasp hands with Hood.

"Damn, you got dude checking me for weapons like he a bouncer at a club now?" Hood said with an annoyed tone. He mean mugged me as he gave Scorch a bro-hug. "Long time, no see, fam."

I smirked at him and nonchalantly sipped from my drink. It was too late to back out now. I would just have to play it cool and hope shit didn't blowup in my face.

"Just taking the necessary precautions to protect myself." Scorch pulled away from the embrace and put some distance between himself and Hood. Byron stood behind him with his arms folded. "Some very disturbing allegations have been brought to my attention concerning you, my man."

Hood's face twisted. "What're you talking about?"

"Wicked here tells me that you and Max were conspiring to take me out." His eyes narrowed into a burning gaze. "Is that true?"

"What??? That's bullshit!" Hood growled, leering at me. "You gonna believe this newbie nigga? I've been here from the beginning, yo!"

"And the serpent was in the Garden of Eden from the beginning too," Scorch replied sarcastically.

"I can't believe this shit, man." Hood's denial was so convincing, I almost believed it myself for a second. "You must've forgot it was my street connects that helped you start this label and get the whole trafficking operation we got going on off the ground?"

"I haven't forgotten anything. I'm well aware of your contribution to The Fiyah Spitta Family. But you still haven't answered the question: Are you, or are you not working with people to take me out?" He stared Hood in the eye.

"I was supposed to be a silent partner in this shit, man." Hood squared up with him. "The music side and the drug side. But you've been fucking me over for years and thought I was too stupid to realize it. So yeah...yeah it's true."

Scorch shook his head. "Damn, no loyalty whatsoever."

"Nigga, fuck outta here. Your greedy ass is the one who's disloyal! When we started this shit, you were only supposed to be the public face of the company to give it corporate legitimacy, while I gave it street credibility."

I was just sitting there like a fly on the wall taking all this in. I'd followed these dudes' careers for years, but to my knowledge, it'd never been publically reported that they had an arrangement similar to the one Dame Dash and Jay-Z used to have with Roc-a-Fella Records. Hood had lied to me big time. He wasn't just a disgruntled talent like he claimed; he was a silent partner in the company who apparently was tired of being silent.

"Over the years, you let all this money and power go to your head," Hood continued. "Your bitchass wasn't nothing but an empty suit with no heart for all the real, gritty parts of the game. But now you think you're a kingpin and shit, calling shots and ordering hits. Paying niggas to watch all of us like hawks and keep tabs on us. You may have sent some goons after Max, but trust and believe, that shit won't happen to--" Scorch pimp slapped him before he could finish his sentence.

"Watch your fucking mouth before you end up just like him," he snapped. "Regardless of how it all started, I and I alone run things around here now. Got it?"

Hood rubbed his jaw, his face balled up with contempt. "Fuck you, son."

Scorch looked at him with an eerily calm expression. "It's been nice doing business with you, Hood. But as of now, our partnership is over. Effective immediately, your contract and your life are terminated. Byron, get this ignorant ingrate out of my presence." He snapped his fingers. Apparently, that was the cue for Byron to escort Hood out. Scorch stood there confidently, waiting for Byron to act.

Hood reached in his leather jacket and pulled out a gun.

A look of panic and fear washed over Scorch's face.

Hood aimed the gun at him and fired two shots.

He fell to the ground, clutching his chest.

"I didn't want to get my hands dirty, but oh well. It's not the first time I had to body someone who got outta line. A nigga didn't get to where is by not being ruthless."

"Byron...help me," Scorch said weakly, his mouth bloody. He struggled to extend a hand towards his bodyguard's ankle.

Byron looked down at him with a blank face as he casually pulled a gun from his coat and put a bullet in Scorch's head.

"That's what I'm talking about, son." Hood snickered, a smug grin playing at his lips. "Earn that paycheck! Scorch paid you well, but now that he's out the way and I own one hundred percent of this operation, I'm going to pay you better. Now you won't have to worry about some egomaniac always telling you what to do, either." The grin vanished from his face when he turned to me. "If you had been smart and went along, you could've been a part of the new Scorcher Records, mah dude." He paused and twisted his lips in contemplation. "Hmm...maybe I'll rename it 'Hood Records' now."

I just sat there watching all of this unfold like it was a movie. Everything had spiraled out of control so fast. All of this definitely wasn't part of the plan.

"Nigga, are you crazy???" I blurted out without thinking. "There's probably security cameras all over this joint. You'll never get away with this!"

"Me and Big By know this place inside and out. All the video can be erased, and our tracks easily covered. This nigga has so many enemies, the cops will be investigating this shit forever and still never find out who did it." He laughed. "Now, all we need to do is tie up the loose end: You."

Before Hood could level his Glock at me, I sprung from the sofa, tackling him to the floor. We started wrestling for the gun. I almost managed to grab it until I was snatched off of him. Byron spun me around and then punched me in the face. Dazed, I staggered backwards, feeling like I'd just been hit by a 2 X 4. He charged at me and wrapped his big hands around my neck. I fumbled behind me, trying to grab anything I could to use as a weapon. My hand brushed against something that felt like a vase on the fireplace mantle. I grabbed it and smashed him over his bald head with it.

Glass shattered everywhere.

Byron's dome started leaking, but that didn't stop him from trying to choke the life out of me. He lifted me off the floor. I gasped for breath as my feet dangled in the air. I kneed him in his nuts twice. He grunted and slammed me down through the glass table, shattering it. I could feel shards of glass sticking me in the back. I just laid there, groaning in pain. I turned my head to see Byron's feet approaching. My vision was blurry. I fought the urge to black out. I knew if I closed my eyes, I would never open them again. It took all my strength to stumble to my feet. I suddenly felt the cold barrel of a gun at my temple.

"Game over, bruh."

I reluctantly looked up into Hood's face. His eyes were cold and lifeless.

"You 'bout to pay for crossing me."

"Whatever, yo. If you gonna do it, then do it. Miss me with all the bullshit and get it over with." I stared back at him with contempt. If I was going down, it wouldn't be like a bitch. I regretted a lot of things in my life, but none more than the realization that I wouldn't be around to see my son grow up. I'd lied to him. I wasn't going to be in his life like I'd said. Hopefully, he would be able to forgive me for breaking my promise when he was older. I gritted my teeth, waiting for the end.

A loud crash suddenly came from somewhere else in the house.

"What the fuck???" Hood looked in the direction of the noise. In a matter of seconds, a SWAT team stormed into the room wearing bulletproof vests with their guns drawn.

"Drop the weapon! Now!!!" One of them yelled.

Hood clenched his jaw and looked down at me, his eye twitching. For a second, it looked as if he was weighing his options. It didn't take him long to come to the conclusion that he had none. He reluctantly set his gun on the floor and raised his hands above his heard. Byron did the same.

Once they were both secured and being led away, Detective Lamar and Agent Myers entered the room.

"Are you okay?" Myers asked, his concern clearly fake.

"Yeah, I'm fine." I rose to my feet. "Considering you guys almost got me killed."

"We were parked in the neighborhood monitoring everything via your wire," he said. "You weren't in any real danger."

"Damn, could've fooled me." I looked around at all the carnage and winched at the sharp pain in my back. "To be so close by, you sure took your sweet time gettin' here." I rubbed at my chest, feeling the wire that had been taped to it prior to my release from jail.

"Unfortunately, we couldn't just kick the door down and barge in without a warrant. We had to wait until there was probable cause before we could enter. The gunshots we heard were all the probable cause we needed." Lamar glanced down and frowned.

"Yeah, whatever," I mumbled, my eyes following his gaze to Scorch's lifeless body. The EMT's had already given up on him. His shirt was open and his bloody chest exposed. The platinum dragon medallion which once hung from his neck rested beside him. It was covered with his blood. I turned my head. I never imagined my ambitions to be a rapper would lead to this. I saw shades of myself in Scorch and Hood, and it saddened and sickened me. I never wanted to become ruthless and heartless like them. We human beings were capable of doing some foul shit when we allowed our greed and desires to control us. I removed my own necklace that Scorch had given me the day I signed, and dropped it to the floor. Although things hadn't gone as planned, I was just glad it was all over.

EPILOGUE

I stood at the window looking down at the city below. The light of the full moon reflected on my naked body. A month had passed since Scorch's death and Hood's and Byron's arrests, but I was still shaken and haunted by that night. I felt a pair of strong arms wrap around my waist. A warm, bare chest pressed up against my back.

"What's wrong?" His deep, soothing voice whispered in my ear.

"Nothin'. Just thinkin'."

He rubbed a hand over my abs. "About...?"

I didn't reply.

"No more secrets, remember?"

"I know." I sighed, lowering my head. Every aspect of my life had been turned upside down over the last couple months. Hood and Byron were both currently locked up awaiting trial. In exchange for my cooperation, I wasn't goin' to receive any time for the gun charge. However, I still wasn't out of the woods yet. Once they went to trial, I would undoubtedly be expected to testify for the prosecution. "I'm just worried about the future, yo."

"I feel you." His strong hands turned me around to face him. "But you don't need to be worried. It's all gonna be OK." Max gave me a reassuring smile. I smiled back at him weakly. I thanked God every day that he'd pulled through his ordeal and was still here. We were back together, but there were times I wondered if we could ever be the way we were before all of this. He lifted my chin with his fingers and stared into my eyes. "Do you trust me, baby?"

I smiled again, this time more earnestly. "Yeah, I trust you with my life, mah dude." After he got out the hospital, he told me the full story about how Hood had recruited him because he knew he was against Scorch, too. He was soon approached by the feds, who revealed they were also working to take Scorch down. They proceeded to put pressure on Max to work with them and keep it on the hush. This being a highly secret and intricate sting operation, he wasn't allowed to tell anyone about his involvement, including me.

He admitted that still didn't excuse him from not trusting me enough to tell me about Scorch earlier. And for my part, I admitted I was wrong for going behind his back the way I had to get a record deal.

That was all in the past now.

"Good. I feel the same way." He leaned in and kissed me. "As long as we got each other and trust, that's all we need. It's all about me and you from now on, kid."

"Just like old times, huh?" I chuckled.

"Yep." He kissed me again. "Just like old times, baby."

"I hope the world is ready for us," I said, kissing him back. "Cause Wicked Will and Madd Maximus--the Dynamic Duo--are about to take over hip-hop."

JUST THE BEGINNING...

Thanks for reading! If you have any questions, comments, or suggestions, feel free to reach out and drop me a line. I appreciate and respond to all feedback. You can find me in the cyberverse on Facebook [ReginaldWrite], Twitter @ReginaldWrite, or on my website, Reginaldwrite.com. Also, (pretty) please be sure to sign up to my email list to receive updates on future releases! LOVE YOU ALL, AND THANKS FOR THE SUPPORT!

OTHER WORKS AVAILABLE BY THIS AUTHOR

Tempted
The Breaking Point
Beyond the Breaking Point
Past the Breaking Point
Teacher's Pet
My Boyfriend's Brother
Playing with Fire
Playing with Fire Pt 2: Friendly Fire
My Son's Teacher

CPSIA information can be obtained
at www.ICGtesting.com
Printed in the USA
LVHW041808160119
604162LV00015B/240/P